The Legend of the Clouds:

Encounter
at
Cloud Ranch

Robert James Connors

Copyright © 2018 Robert James Connors

Susan C. Connors, Senior Editor

ISBN-10: 0-9991904-6-6

ISBN-13: 978-0-9991904-6-3

Published 2018 by

Plumeria Publishing

207 East Park Avenue, Lake Wales, FL 33853

Contents

Legend of the Clouds:

Encounter at Cloud Ranch

Chapter One

AS HE STARED AT THE CARCASS FROM HIS HORSE, Tom Cloud knew that whatever had killed the cow had done a thorough job of it. The spring's melting snows had revealed it at the foot of an arroyo that sloped through Tom's ranch from the cliffs above. Tying his horse to a piñon pine, he slowly picked his way up the cleft in the polished sandstone toward the remains.

Tom had grown up on the ranch, an inheritance from his father, but he had never grown tired of the spectacular setting. The morning sun illuminated the multi-colored face of dramatic cliffs that soared into the sky above him. Below, his ranch was mostly parched rangeland, happily watered by a small, seasonal creek and the pumping of windlasses. Today he faced another of the many problems that his years of ranching had made all too familiar.

He bent to examine the remains. The skull of the cow was visible, still partly covered in brown hide. Other bones had been scattered by animals. It was a puzzle. Above him the cliffs of slickrock sandstone made an effective barrier to rustlers. There was no sign anyone had been around, but plenty of possible perpetrators came to his mind, both human and otherwise. He turned the facts over in his mind as he rode back to the spacious house on his C9 Ranch.

"I was out looking for some strays this morning, my new hired hands haven't quite got things under control yet," Tom told his son Jason that evening over dinner. "I had already searched all the fences in the truck and had to finish along the cliffs on horseback. It's a good thing we don't run any more land out that way, I couldn't afford to fence it all."

"I wish I had gotten back home yesterday, then," Jason replied. "I could have ridden with you."

"Well, it wouldn't have really been your line of studies. I don't think 'Forensic Anthropology' has anything to do with animals. Still, you might have found it interesting, knowing you as I do. I found one cow that looked like it had been killed by something a few weeks back. I don't know what it could have been, but it was cut up pretty good."

"Bones are bones with me, Dad. You know that," Jason replied, brushing his thick shock of dark hair away from his eyes. "Remember I was only about four when I found some bones, and you had me try to figure out what kind of animal it was. That's how I got started, and I've been into it ever since."

Tom smiled at the memory. "Strangest thing is," he continued, "I didn't see a sign anyone had crossed a fence, no tracks at all, but it didn't look like an animal kill to me. Some of the large bones had been removed, and I searched the entire area. They were gone. Animals don't do that. They might carry off smaller pieces, but not hundreds of pounds at a time."

Jason glanced at his dad, his fork poised in the air. Tom was 46, sun-browned, and hard as nails from his work on the ranch. Jason had nothing but respect for the man who was his entire family. "Well, I don't have to be back at university for two weeks, Dad," he offered. "I can make time to ride out there and have a look. You've got my curiosity up."

"Fine with me, just be careful," Tom told him.

•

At first light the following morning, Jason was already in the saddle, having grabbed coffee and a muffin to steel himself against the brisk air. His breath hung before him in an icy cloud, but he knew that the rising sun would soon push the chill away for both himself and his horse. He headed west, casting long shadows across a rolling landscape decorated with scattered rabbit bush, apache plume, rosemary-mint, and Indian paintbrush. Above him to the north, the sandstone cliffs rose almost vertically more than two thousand feet, dazzling in the sunlight.

Sunrise was his favorite time of day, and his ride reminded him again just how much he had missed it during his time at college. Jason had always loved the ranch, and as he grew he had learned to handle the ranch operations. By now, he thought, he could do it as well as his dad in a pinch. His dad had always expected him to take over one day, but that expectation had been cast in doubt by his decision to go to college. Jason still felt a sense of guilt, but his father had been supportive every step of the way. He sighed and refocused on the challenge ahead.

The spring calving season was underway, and in the distance, he could see their two new ranch hands riding through the herd, checking the newborn calves and still-pregnant cows for any signs of distress It was a big job covering several thousand acres of ranch, and hired hands were essential. Jason hadn't met the men yet, as they had been hired only weeks earlier after one of their cowhands had gotten married and moved to Albuquerque, and the other retired. Happily, in bad weather the herd tended to gather around feeding stations, which were essential until the summer grasses grew in earnest.

The cliffs had been Jason's youthful hangouts, a fantasy world rippling for countless miles across the northern horizon. In some places the cliff rose almost vertically from the level of the ranch. In others they were footed by slopes of soft talus, a mixture of boulders, stones, gravel, and sand that had weathered off the face of the cliff. There he had learned to rock-climb and had spent many summer mornings scaling the slickrock.

On many days he had scaled the cliffs just to enjoy the reward of spectacular views over their ranch stretching down the valley, and the thread of the streambed, marked by scattered cottonwood and tamarisk trees. He knew the cliff faces by heart, and if someone had gone in to any of the dozens of deep clefts that cut their faces, he would find the evidence. Jason knew it would take men with a truck to haul cattle off the ranch. Unseen? Impossible, he thought.

Jason tethered his horse and crept a short distance up the slope of talus his father had described. Today he would need no ropes or pitons to climb. He would only walk on the bottom edge of the rubble. The stones there had been tumbled and polished by the minor flows which often followed rain on the high country. On those days, a heavy storm could turn some of the narrow arroyos into cascading streams and waterfalls, but today they were dry. He climbed at last to a bed of small stones that crunched under his boots as he approached the carcass.

He found the remains of the cow partially shaded by a pine tree, and partly hidden by an outcropping rib of rock. It took Jason only a moment to see why his dad had been stumped. The bones lay together, but he realized with a start that the skeleton was incomplete. He bent down to take a closer look. It ended in a neat cut about a foot behind the shoulders. It was less than half a cow. He cast about the area and found no sign of the rest.

Jason walked higher up the arroyo, leaving the skeleton of the unfortunate cow behind him. His horse gave a soft whinny as he walked away, but he reassured it with a few soft words. It was too cold for rattlesnakes, which were still in hibernation, but he wore a revolver in case of other trouble. His eyes roamed the rocky walls and the path before his feet, refreshing his memories of the place. Almost every stone seemed familiar. He cast back and forth searching the ground until at last his eye caught a glimpse of bleached white bone. Probably too old to be the cow, he thought. He stepped up on a larger rock to get a good look and saw a curved shape, perhaps a pelvic bone, or even a skull. 'Enough to make identification simple,' he told himself. 'Likely it's a bighorn sheep or coyote.'

Climbing down, he pushed the shape with his boot. It rolled loose from its half-buried position and flipped over. He could see it was only a partial upper skull, but it was almost a foot long. The lower jaw and upper right side were missing. He tried to compare it to what he knew of animal physiology. A bear? No, wrong sort of jaws. Shaped too round to be deer. Pretty much too large for anything else likely to be around. The pumas weren't that big...

He carefully brushed off some of the dried mud and saw that it still had a row of upper teeth, or... He realized with a start that what should be a row of teeth seemed to be fused into a single large tooth, almost like a saw blade. There was a single long fang protruding downward at the front, where it seemed that the jaw would normally re-curve. Jason bent down and touched it. Smooth bone met his fingers, but the texture was strange It wasn't fossilized, but it had a sort of metallic feel to it. What appeared to be the top of the skull had a bulge, he realized, but no sign of horns or antlers. It certainly wasn't prehistoric, but it was strange enough that it raised his curiosity.

Jason glanced around at the red sandstone 'slickrock' that formed the backdrop. Nothing else seemed out of the ordinary, but there was something about this bone that gave him a sense of unease. How had it gotten here, he wondered? It was question he was going to answer.

It took him ten minutes to get back to his horse and return with a plastic rain poncho and a small blanket. He carefully retrieved the skull and wrapped in it the two layers of fabric, tying it with a length of thin leather from his saddlebags. He then put the cord over his shoulder and climbed back down the slope to his horse.

Arriving back at the ranch house a short while later, his father met him in the barn as he was putting away his saddle. "I got some bad news a few minutes ago," Tom told him. "Billy Horton called. He's the undertaker, remember? He told me that Richard Martin died last night."

Jason knew both the men. Richard Martin had visited many times since he took over the neighboring ranch a few years earlier. He also remembered the undertaker. He had hoped he would never have to see him again. Jason had been only 14 when his mother had passed away, the most traumatic event of his life. Now tragedy had reopened the pain of those memories.

"That's terrible," Jason replied. "How did he die? He was only in his early thirties, and he seemed really healthy."

"I don't know," Tom said. "Billy told me that there's no obvious reason, but he doubles as the county coroner, so I guess he's going to have to try to figure it out. He also told me Ashley found him on the ground last night. I'm sure that wasn't an easy thing for her. I'm heading over there in a while to see her. You're welcome to come along."

At the mention of Ashley, Jason's thoughts jumped to Richard's young wife, suddenly a widow. He'd carried a torch for her since she had taught his English class when he was fifteen. She had been fresh from college, and made his heart skip a beat. She was petite, blonde, and polished, an easterner in a western world. He had been a guest at her marriage to Richard only a year earlier, and now she was alone again. He chided himself for thinking of her in that way at a moment like this.

"Thanks, Dad. Of course, I'll come. Give me a little while to get cleaned up."

"I've asked Juanita to make up a basket of food to bring over," his father told him. "There's a cake coming out of the oven in half-an-hour, if that's enough time for you." Jason knew that Juanita, their Latina housekeeper, could whip up the best cakes and pies in six counties, and some of the most satisfying meals he had ever eaten. It would be comfort food for mourners.

•

The gravel road to the Martin's neighboring Circle M ranch took them along a mile of their own fence-line, dipping through two dry washes along the way. After a storm they might contain torrents, and the potholes in the road reminded them of past wash-outs. Ten minutes brought them to the long drive that led back north toward the sprawling ranch house and its flanking barns. They passed a couple of empty hay and cattle trailers and drove into the dusty front yard. It was not a surprise that there were no other visitors parked there. In the isolated life of ranching in the Four Corners area, neighbors were scarce.

A long porch fronted the house, and at their approach Ashley Martin opened the door in the shade of the overhanging roof. "Please come in, gentlemen," she said as they mounted the steps. "You've likely heard my terrible news," she added, and then began to sob.

As Tom reached her, he extended his hand, and she fell against him, her crying intensifying. He instinctively wrapped his arms around her and attempted to calm her. Jason felt a twinge of jealousy, but then stopped himself, realizing that his father, himself a widower, understood as well as anyone the pain of losing a spouse. He looked down at the large picnic basket and tried to keep his mind away from the fragile figure of Ashley.

Seated in the living room a short while later, Ashley told them she wanted to share her story because it didn't make any sense. She spoke calmly about what had happened, how Richard had gone out to the barn to check on the horses. She suspected his reason was really to sneak a smoke, as he had promised to quit, but was struggling to do so. When he didn't come back after half an hour, she had called him, and finally gone out to look for him. She had found him on the ground. As she spoke, she stared out the broad front windows to distant mountains, blue through the haze to the southwest. Jason tried not to stare as well, but it was Ashley herself that distracted him.

Eventually they turned the conversation away from the tragedy, and onto the doings on the ranch. All had been going "fairly well," she said. They hadn't lost any cows through the winter, but Richard had recently found two head of cattle that had been killed near the cliffs. Both had been butchered, and he had told her he suspected some hermit living up on the mountain had done the deed, because there was no sign of tire tracks.

"That's strange, because I found one yesterday, pretty much the same situation," Tom told her. "Jason rode out there this morning to check it out. You know he's studying bones in college."

"Yes, that's right," Ashley said. "I had forgotten what he had chosen as his major, but I always knew he would do well. He's a brilliant student."

Jason blushed slightly, embarrassed to have her speak about him, and swiftly changed the subject, asking for more details about the bones. She had none to offer. "Would you mind if I rode over in the next day or two and scouted along the cliffs?" he asked as they were leaving. "I'd like to compare your lost cattle to ours and inspect the scene. I might be able to learn something about who's taking them."

"I would be very grateful if you would, Jason. Thank you so much for caring," she replied, giving him the briefest of half-smiles.

•

The silence of the drive back home was broken when Jason spoke up, after turning a question in his mind. "Dad, I hadn't told you about what I found out there this morning. You were right about that cow. It looked like two thirds of it was just gone. There was no sign of any people, or even animals, for that matter, except for a strange skull I found. I can't tell what it is, and I'm pretty good about that. Would you mind taking a look at it?"

"Of course. I don't know if I can add anything," Tom replied. "You're way better'n me at figuring that out now. Do you think it has anything to do with the cattle?"

"That's not likely, it's pretty old. But I will tell you that anything that can make off with a thousand pounds of beef and not leave tracks has got me stumped."

•

After dinner that evening Jason unwrapped his relic, and the two men examined it for a few minutes. Both marveled at what seemed to be the deformed tooth, and the long fang that was still embedded in the skull. The saw-blade tooth was fully five inches long, and the exposed part of the fang nearly the same length. It was a formidable-looking bite, whatever it was.

"You're sure it's not prehistoric?" Tom asked his son, and got assurances that it was bone, not fossil, and probably not more than a few years old.

"It's like nothing I ever heard about living in these mountains in all my years, except maybe in the wild tales 'Chopper' Jones used to tell," Tom told him.

"Wasn't he the Korean war vet? I remember him from when I was a kid."

"Yeah, he used to tell wild tales of a beast of some sort living up on the plateau. Nobody really believed him, though. He disappeared into the mountains about a dozen years back, when you were still in junior high, I think. Isadora used to warn me not to hang around him, or people would think I was crazy, too," he said with a chuckle. "God, I still miss your mom."

"I do too, Dad. She was good for both of us."

•

The next day was Saturday, and Jason took advantage of warmer weather to take his promised ride along Ashley's ranch. Since the two ranches were adjacent, all it required was for him to open a gate in the shared barbed wire fence that divided the properties. As a gate it was not much, just an extra fence-post with a piece of baling-wire that held it in place, allowing the three strands of barbed-wire to fold back to let his horse through. He headed on east along the foot of the mesa, the enormous cliffs parting from time to time to reveal the deep arroyos cut into their flanks. Jason turned his horse into each in sequence and dismounted to search. He found nothing that might lead him to climb more than a hundred feet up each draw.

In the distance he could see the barns behind Ashley's ranch-house. He had already ridden to the far end of the ranch and was about to turn around when he finally spotted the bones of a cow hidden in some brush. He immediately dismounted and began to cast about in search of any tracks. Hoof-prints of a horse were obvious, and he assumed that they had been left by Richard's visit to the scene less than a week earlier. He pulled out his cell phone and took a few photos, to compare the prints with Richard's horse later. Then he approached the bones.

As on his own ranch, the cow had been sliced up. This time there was a clean cut, two feet from the rump, but he noticed that several ribs were also cut from the spine on one side. He bent to examine the cuts. 'Clean as a whistle!' he remarked to himself. They looked as if they had been done with a power saw. Someone had made off with almost an entire side of beef and had done it in a professional manner. If there was a hermit living in the mountains, he must be a fugitive surgeon, he thought.

Jason had remounted and was ready to resume searching the flank of the mesa when he spotted something that made him stop. A strange hole had been dug, partially hidden by a large rock. It was almost three feet across, and as he looked into the sloping cavity, he realized that it was more than ten feet deep. The excavated material had been scattered, almost as if it were being hidden among the boulders. The ground here at the foot of the cliffs was still more stony talus that had eroded from far above and collected at the bottom. He had known bears to den in the mountains, and sometimes close to the ranch, but they normally used natural cavities. He had never known one to carry out an excavation of this size.

He was still poking around when he heard a horse approaching. He stood and was pleased to see that it was Ashley, riding her favorite paint. The sunlight behind her made a halo of her blonde hair.

"Hello, Jason. I hope I'm not interrupting," came Ashley's soft voice as she reined her horse. Jason shivered slightly and smiled up at her.

"Not at all," he replied. "'I'm very glad to see you. I was just trying to figure out what dug this hole. It's pretty deep. None of your boys are trying for a well, or a gold mine, are they?"

Ashley smiled back at him, and her long hair swung as she turned her horse. "Not a chance. They do only what we pay them for..." She paused a moment after she realized she had said 'we.' Adapting to her new reality was going to be a painful shift, but she was determined.

"I don't want to slow you down," she continued, "but I saw you from the barn, and thought I'd ride out and thank you again for investigating for me. You are really sweet to help out like this."

Jason swallowed, and tried to retain his composure. "Thank you, Ma'am," he replied.

"Please, Jason, call me Ashley. I'm not your school teacher anymore."

"Sure...Ashley..." Jason tried not to show his reaction, having never had much chance to talk to Ashley before on such a personal level. "Uh, I'm glad you came out," he stammered. "I was, um, I was trying to figure out what this hole was, and whether it had anything to do with your cow over there," he said, nodding in the direction of the partial skeleton, now hidden in the brush. "It sure looks like it wasn't an animal. The spine is cut as clean as any butcher's saw could do it."

"Chuck and Mosely found that cow last week, but never mentioned anything strange about it to me," Ashley replied with a frown. "Maybe they told Richard."

Jason had met the two hired hands several times. Both were professional cowmen who could lasso and brand a calf in a minute. He wished his dad had had as much success hiring hands for their ranch.

"Richard had found another one, not too far up that way," Ashley added, nodding toward the east.

"Well, it's the same thing I saw with the cow on our land," Jason said. "Somebody has apparently found a way down from that mesa and figured out how to steal some beef."

"But then how did they get it back up there?" Ashley asked him. "You don't just throw a cow over your shoulder and climb up a cliff!"

Jason nodded. "That's what I told my Dad, but I'll be danged if I can find another explanation. It wasn't any animal that killed these cattle, that's for sure, and there's no sign that anybody brought a truck out here on our ranches. They'd have been spotted, anyway, and there would be tire tracks. There must be some way they are hauling stuff up these cliffs. Maybe a winch, I don't know, but I would think that would leave some sort of marks, 'cause you'd be dragging it over the rock. If that's the case, I think I'll be able to figure it out. I'm planning to do a little bit of rock climbing the next few days."

"Please be careful, Jason. I don't know what I'd do if something were to happen to you, too," Ashley said seriously.

Jason paused. "Don't worry, Ashley," he told her. "I can take care of myself, and my friends, too, if need be."

"I'm sure you can, Jason, but if there's someone up there, you shouldn't have to confront them alone," Ashley said, and then paused a moment before adding "I should tell you that we are having services for Richard on Tuesday. I hope you can come."

"Of course, Ashley, I wouldn't think of not being there...for you," Jason replied.

"Thank you. I'll see you then," she said, and turned her horse to go.

"It was very nice speaking with you, Ashley," Jason said as she started to ride. She raised her hand in a sort of wave and trotted back down the trail toward her home.

Jason stood for a long moment watching her go. His close encounter had only served to stoke his dreams, but he wasn't sure if she had really said what he thought he had heard. He pondered the exchange a few minutes before he was able to refocus his attention on the question at hand.

Bending back down to inspect the hole, he peered into the dark interior. He thought he detected a whiff of an animal smell, along with the musty smell of earth. He pulled out his phone and used the flashlight, but it did little to illuminate the depths. Inspecting the area, he realized that whatever had dug this burrow, if that's what it was, had moved plenty of large boulders. 'This one must weigh a few hundred pounds!' he thought to himself, pushing against it. It was then that he noticed the strange scratches on the stone. Looking closer, he could see that they were shallow grooves, which seemed to have been cut into the stone by some sort of tool. He looked around and noticed others around the opening.

Crawling on his knees in the soft, churned earth, he began to probe deeper into the hole with his light, closely examining the loose soil for tracks. Then he saw them. Three deep imprints in series, like something had stepped through. Each mark was nearly round, but featured radiating marks all around, almost like a sea star. 'How odd is that?' he thought. 'Could they be footprints?' He counted. Each mark featured seven rounded 'toes,' if that's what they were. A shiver again ran up his spine. There was something very strange going on here, he thought.

Jason backed out of the hole a bit faster than he had entered, stood and looked around cautiously. Whatever had made those prints wasn't like anything he'd ever known. The hair on his neck was standing up as he quickly mounted his horse and rode back toward home.

Chapter Two

"**I** KNOW YOU WERE GOOD FRIENDS, but sometimes these things really can't be explained," Billy Horton said with a shrug. "We couldn't find a thing. No wounds, nothing in the blood, no sign of a stroke, either," he added. "I just have to call it heart failure, even though there was no sign of any heart problems in the autopsy. You know he was a smoker, but that wasn't what killed him. Seems like his heart just stopped beating, and he collapsed. The state coroner couldn't find anything more."

Jason glanced at his dad, wondering if he had the same questions kicking around in his head. Tom just nodded, seeming to accept the answer. Serving as both the county coroner and only undertaker in this isolated place made Horton the local go-to expert on death, and his word was rarely disputed.

"Mr. Horton," Jason began, "could someone's heart be made to stop just because of some sudden shock, like a fright?"

"Well, I wouldn't say it's impossible, but it's certainly rare," he replied. "The usual reaction is 'fight or flight'. Your body produces a big shot of adrenaline, which does rev up your heart, but it shouldn't stop it. Of course, if you already had heart troubles, might be different..."

"So being 'scared to death' is just an expression?" Jason asked.

"I'd have to say yes. I've never seen anything scary enough to kill a healthy man, but then, maybe I've led a sheltered life!" he chuckled in irony, and Jason and Tom joined him. "Well, I'm sorry we don't have anything more definitive to give Mrs. Martin closure, but that's all there is, and I can't make up evidence. She took it well enough. She's a strong young woman."

"I thank you for stopping by and letting us know, Billy," Tom said as they rose from their chairs. "I guess we'll see you at the service tomorrow."

"Alright, then. Tomorrow," Horton said, quickly picking up his hat and heading out the door.

Tom and Jason watched him get into his truck in the evening light before either one spoke.

"I can't help feeling that there must be more to Richard just dying so suddenly," Jason said.

"We'll probably never know anything more about it than we do right now," Tom said, and turned to the bar that stood at one end of the large living room. He brought down a glass and poured himself an ounce of Irish whiskey, something he'd learned to enjoy in the service. Jason sat turning over the eventful few days since his return from college. It seemed that things were challenging some long-held beliefs.

"Dad, do you think there was any chance that Chopper Jones really had seen something living in those cliffs?" Jason asked. "I mean, the cut-up cows, the strange den, and the tracks, that tells me that there's something weird going on. I don't know if Richard's death is connected in any way, but it just seems really abnormal..."

"Well, don't let your imagination run away with you, son. There's some strange things in this world, for sure, but most often there's a more common explanation."

"I guess you're right," Jason admitted." "If I'm going to be a scientist, I'd better stick to facts, not conjecture."

14

"Just don't start any rumors," Tom told him. "It's hard enough to keep help around here now. One of my new hands quit today, said he couldn't work with the other man."

"I'm sorry I'm not around more to help, Dad. I know how much work there is in this place."

"No, you need to concentrate on your studies, make it all worthwhile," Tom replied. "This place will still be here later on."

"Thanks, Dad. Well, if you don't mind, I think I'll go hit the books for a while, and then turn in early," Jason said. "We've got to be at the funeral home at ten."

"Goodnight, Jason. See you in the morning."

•

Jason tried to study, but his mind kept wandering back to the strange clues. It was a mystery he intended to solve. He suddenly remembered the strange partial skull and added that to the growing pile of evidence. Something odd was going on, and it seemed to involve an unknown sort of animal. Rising, he walked to his dresser and picked up the loosely-wrapped bundle, peeling back the cloth to reveal the strange fang and tooth. It was only the front and upper part of a skull, so he could see no way of knowing how much of it was missing. Maybe he should take it with him to the university, he thought, and let his instructors have a look at it. Maybe his professor could explain what he had found. With that thought he pulled out his phone and took several photos and emailed them to his instructor with a brief description and a few questions. At last he folded the cloth back over the macabre skull and readied himself for bed.

•

An almost moonless night left Jason's room in near-total darkness, with only starlight entering through the broad windows, but for Jason that was enough. He eyes quickly adjusted to faint light, and something had disturbed him. Always a light sleeper, he could easily ignore the familiar songs of the coyotes or the hoot of an owl. This was something different.

Motionless, he peered around the room from under his blanket. Something, he could swear, had moved in his room. He watched intently, trying to convince himself not to close his eyes and go back to sleep.

15

For three long minutes he watched until his eyelids began to droop, thinking his imagination was too active. Then suddenly he saw something that made his skin crawl. A strange distortion became apparent as objects in the room seemed to shift slightly, as if caused by the passage of a sort of wave in front of them. As he watched, he began to make out the shape of a sphere, almost like a soap-bubble, that was moving in the room. About a foot across, it seemed to somehow mask its passage and was almost invisible, but he was certain it was real.

With a sudden leap Jason sprang from the bed and flipped on the light, hoping to get a better look, but in that instant, it had disappeared. He cast about the room, looking for it. The windows were closed tightly against the chill, and his bedroom door was also pulled tight. There was no way in or out, but he was sure he had seen it, wasn't he? A tiny doubt crept into his mind. 'Was I dreaming?'

Feeling like a child afraid of monsters, he checked the closet and under the bed. There was no sign of any sphere, transparent or otherwise. He scratched his head. What could it have been? Then his eyes fell upon the cloth on his dresser, now a limp pile. He dashed to unwrap it and found nothing but cloth. The skull was gone.

Was it possible? No one had been in the room, and he hadn't left. He dashed out of the bedroom, turning on lights as he ran. The house was empty. The exterior floodlights revealed nothing. Returning to his room, Jason pondered this strange event for an hour. Sleep was scarce that night.

Chapter Three

WEDNESDAY WAS ANOTHER SUNNY DAY, typical of spring in the Four Corners region of Colorado, New Mexico, Arizona, and Utah. Jason had seen Ashley at the reception that followed the somber ceremony of the funeral the day before and was glad to see that she was composed and coping with her loss. Now he was ready to clear his mind and get out into nature again, to try to answer the questions still burning in his head. He would use his rudimentary science training to identify what sort of animal had been able to haul so much beef up the imposing cliffs.

Jason's determination to solve the mystery had only deepened since the appearance of the apparition in his room, and the sudden disappearance of the skull. He had hesitated to mention those facts to his father, for fear of having him call a halt to his investigations. Some things are better done alone, he thought.

As he rode he made it a point to enjoy the scenery and the fresh scent of the scattered piñon pines and Utah juniper. The first of the spring flowers were just starting to emerge, flecks of orange from the desert globemallow making only a slight contrast with the red-tinted sands. The long, curving line of the plateau face was an enchantment for the few summertime visitors to the area, with its woven layers of red and yellow sandstone. The remains of those ancient, fossilized sand dunes had been cut by rain and polished by wind to form a striking display that ran for many miles, a natural barrier to northward movement. Although some called it a mesa, he knew that it was just one step of the *Escalante*, the 'Grand Staircase' of steps that rise from the southern deserts to the heights of the Colorado Plateau, which sprawled across the Four Corners region. Today, he would explore one tiny part of that massive formation.

A few hours later, he was deep into his work. The sheer face of the escarpment loomed above as Jason clung to the slickrock a hundred feet above the talus slope. He was a bit higher than he had been before on this particular face. It was a difficult climb, but he was enjoying himself. On the way up, he had used a brush to clear sand from questionable handholds and taken the time to replace a couple of 'permanent' pitons he had placed years earlier.

Moving carefully, Jason slowly turned, his arms thrust against the walls of stone on either side of him. There were few places to gain a handhold or foothold, so for security he relied on his harness, and the ropes which were attached to the cams he had carefully placed in narrow cracks. Dangling with his back to the smooth stone, he looked back down at the distance he had come, over hundreds of yards of boulders and talus rubble, and another hundred feet up the slickrock. From this height Jason could see most of the C9 Ranch spread out below, the red earth speckled with mesquite bushes and cattle. To his left he could see the roofs of Ashley's barns.

The climb had been as exhilarating as it was strenuous, but it had yielded no evidence of anything out of the ordinary. He was puzzled. He was sure that anyone dragging heavy loads of beef up the cliffs would have had to use one of these clefts, where the activity would be at least partially hidden. He studied the rock above and around him. There were no other obvious routes. If someone had been moving up and down this section of the cliffs, it could only have been an experienced rock climber, yet not a trace of man or animal was to be seen. Perhaps this whole expedition was a wild goose-chase, and he should try other angles, he thought to himself, as he prepared to make his decent.

It was then that he spotted something beneath him that had somehow escaped notice on the way up. Probably because he had been so focused on where to place his hands and feet, he had overlooked the circular opening only a few yards away from his path. An outcrop in the wavy folds of eroded stone kept it hidden from below.

Jason was puzzled. If it was a mine, he thought, it was a strange place for one. What was it doing up here, in the cliff face? How did the miners get to it? There had never been any evidence of steps, or a sluice, or even water to pan out any fines. He knew that some of the nearby mountains were riddled with old gold and silver mines. Prospecting had arrived in a wave, but very few places had produced any significant amounts of ore. Most had been wasted time. A mine here didn't make sense at all.

Jason kept his back to the rock and sidled slowly to his left, his rubber boot-soles clinging to the barest of rough places. After two anxious minutes he reached the opening, gripped its edge, and hoisted himself inside.

When he had caught his breath, Jason began to examine the shaft. It certainly wasn't natural, he realized. Perfectly circular, the walls were smoother than the weathered cliff-face outside and ran as straight as an arrow into the mountain. It was level and tall enough to stand in. Jason flipped on his phone flashlight and took a few steps forward, examining the surface of the tunnel. 'Almost polished!' he thought to himself. Then he noticed something else out of the ordinary. A light breeze was entering the shaft from behind him. 'It's not just a short tunnel, it must have another opening,' he thought.

Determined to find out more, Jason released his carabiners and began to walk slowly forward, until the light of the opening was all but lost, a tiny disc in the distance. He estimated that he was well over a hundred yards in, and realized that he should have counted his steps, but still the tunnel continued straight as an arrow, and still he detected the same breeze. Not the musty smell of a cave, but fresh air. And, he noted, bone dry. No seepage of moisture came from the walls or ceiling, and there was nothing trickling at his feet, either.

Another few hundred steps showed him no variation in the tunnel, and Jason began to think about turning back. He had a sudden realization that if something happened to him in there, no one would ever know. He took another step forward, and suddenly stopped. The low ceiling had disappeared, and now, he realized, so had the walls. He shined the light downward again and saw nothing but blackness. He backed up a step and dropped to his knees, and his fingers felt along the sharp edge of an abyss. His circular tunnel had intersected a vertical shaft, leaving a sharply-chiseled edge. With a start he realized that his tunnel didn't have a ventilation shaft, it *was* a ventilation shaft. That's why there was no easy access from the cliff face. None was needed. So, he realized, there must be another entrance to the shaft.

He shined his feeble light into the darkness but saw no sign of a far wall. Above his head the shaft seemed to continue upward. How deep could it be? Jason fumbled around for a small stone to toss, but the tunnel was clean, almost as if it were swept. He dug in his pockets for a coin but found only a single bullet, meant for his .45 revolver. 'That'll work,' he thought to himself, and with a forceful backhand flip he cast it hard into the darkness. He heard a click of contact from a distant wall, and listened intently for a sound from the depths, but heard nothing. Again he felt the hair on the back of his neck rise, and a chill surged through his body. There was something unearthly about this shaft. It was clearly no ordinary mine, being as much as a hundred feet in diameter. Was it some sort of military relic? A missile silo, perhaps? Could a project so immense have been hidden from generations of local ranchers, excavated right under their noses? He doubted it.

As he sat and pondered the possibilities, he thought he heard, for the first time in the silence of the shaft, a faint plopping sound. Almost like dripping water, but rhythmic, like...slow footfalls. But it was coming from far below, and, he realized with a start, growing closer. There was something down there, and it was climbing.

Jason retraced his steps as quickly as he could and carefully scrambled down the mountain face to his tethered horse. His ride back to the ranch house was filled with conflicting, and frightening, ideas.

Chapter Four

"NO, JASON, I CAN'T SAY I HAVE ANY IDEA just what that is, or was," came the voice from the video link on his notebook. "If I didn't know what a serious student you are, I might think that you were pulling a practical joke of 'stump the professor.'" The image on the screen was one of the photos he had thought to take of the missing skull, zoomed in to show the unusual structure of the tooth.

"No, I wouldn't even consider something so juvenile," Jason replied. "And to be perfectly honest with you, I'm..." he hesitated before adding "worried." Scared would perhaps be more accurate, but he didn't want to seem a coward. "A few other strange things have happened, besides finding this skull, and I'm trying to fit the pieces together. If this is still an extant species, could it be responsible for the slaughter of our cattle?"

"Your cattle are being killed?"

"Professor Thompson, I wish you were here to examine the remains. Their bones have been cut with precision, not shattered at the joints. And it's happening in places no one could get to without being seen by us or our ranch hands, and certainly not with power tools or trucks."

"Do you have photos of that, too?" came the voice from the computer.

Jason flipped through his images until he came to some, and again zoomed in to show the details. "This is probably the best I have, but I can get better, I think. The bones are still out there."

There was a long pause before Professor Thompson spoke again. "Who else has seen these bones?"

"Just myself, my dad, and Richard Martin, I guess, but Richard's dead."

"He's dead?"

"Yes, he died very suddenly, just a few days ago, after he found them on his ranch. They couldn't explain why. He was 34 years old, and healthy, we thought."

"Jason, do me a favor. I'd like to come down there and see this for myself. Do you think you could find me a hotel room someplace nearby?"

"Not a chance. I don't even know of one this side of Cortez," Jason said, "but you can stay here. We have a couple of spare bedrooms."

"Thanks, Jason. That's very kind. Please don't share this with anyone else before I arrive. I'll be there tomorrow."

As the call ended, Jason returned to studying the precision cut of the spine in the image on his computer. It seemed strange to him, and apparently was strange enough to draw a university professor to drive almost three hundred miles to see it in person. He felt a sense of vindication. Calling Anna Thompson had been impulsive, but now he was glad he had acted. Professor Thompson was renowned for her talents, not only in the field of paleontology, but also as a reconstructive expert. She had helped solve crimes by rebuilding faces on old skulls to identify victims, and even had a species of dinosaur named for her after her field work had uncovered a treasure-trove of new fossils in Nebraska. If anyone could tell more about this mystery, it should be her.

There was indeed something very strange about these bones. Jason wondered if he should have told his instructor more about the strange sphere he was sure he had seen, the theft of the skull, or the shaft in the mountain. He hadn't wanted to seem crazy, he thought, so some of that would have to wait.

•

Anna Thompson's mid-day arrival seemed to bring out the best in Tom. She was bright and bubbly, apparently unattached, and at 40, close to Tom's own age. Visitors were rare on the ranch and he insisted on hosting a welcome dinner, asked Juanita to prepare a sumptuous meal, and retrieved a bottle from his wine cellar. Anna seemed flattered but was anxious to see the cattle bones in the light of the afternoon, so before dinner she was mounted alongside Tom and Jason, heading toward the escarpment only a mile from the house. It was a fine spring day, and Tom was pleased to see that she was comfortable in the saddle.

"I found our bones just as the snow was melting," Tom told her. "Jason knows where the others are, on the neighbor's ranch."

"That would be the Martin ranch," Jason added. "The ones that Richard Martin found before he died."

When they reached the bones, Anna quickly set to work, photographing and measuring the site. "Has anyone moved them?" she asked.

"Not intentionally," Jason told her. "I tried not to disturb them when I was taking pictures. There've been a few animals poking around, though."

Anna bent to closely examine the bones and noted the clean cut through the spine. Then she began to measure them carefully, making notes in her small pad for several minutes. Her work complete, the three rode back to the house without further comment about what she had seen.

•

After dinner, Tom suggested a cocktail. "What's your preference?" he asked Anna.

"What are you having?" she asked in return.

"I'm kind'a partial to Tullamore Dew, but I've got some variety."

"I think I'll have what you're having," Anna said. "Rocks would be great."

The three sat on the broad front porch, nursing their drinks and enjoying the still of the evening. An owl hooted in the distance, and a sliver of moon enhanced the fading glow of sunset as the mountains to their south faded into the gloom.

"Thanks for your wonderful hospitality, and that great dinner," Anna said to Tom. "You've really got a beautiful home, and a spectacular setting here."

"Thanks, Anna," Tom replied. "It can be a bit lonesome at times, especially now that Jason is away at the university most of the time. There aren't many people I enjoy talking to, and not many neighbors. One less, now."

"I'm sorry your neighbor died so suddenly," Anna said. "Jason mentioned it on the phone. "Can you tell me any more about that?" Anna asked.

"Not really," Tom replied. "He just collapsed near his barn. His wife found him."

"Was it daylight?" she asked.

"No, it was after dark, I'm pretty sure. Why do you ask?"

"Just curious, I guess. It seems strange, if he was healthy."

"Sound as a dollar, for all everyone knew. The coroner said he couldn't determine the cause of death, except heart failure..."

"My condolences for your loss," Anna said.

"It's a sad thing, for sure, and it's going to be tough on his wife," Tom said. "She's suddenly hung with a large spread to run. Luckily, she's got a couple of good hands on board. They've been there for years and seem to be fiercely loyal to her. I wish I could find some as good," he added. "I lost my hired help a couple of months ago and can't seem to replace them with anyone good. I've got notices posted at several feed stores, and I've used some internet service, but mostly all I find are drifters and rodeo losers. That's the way it goes in the ranching business."

"Well, you've got a beautiful place here, and I hope you find the right help soon. I'd hate to lose Jason as a student and find him out here roping cattle!" Anna teased. "He's got a very bright future, you know."

"I'm sure he does," Tom replied, "and I'm glad that he's not going to be spending his entire life here. There's a big, wide world out there."

Jason squirmed a bit as they spoke, and finally interrupted. "Hey, I'm sitting right here, you know."

Tom laughed. "Oh yeah, you are, aren't you? Well, I wouldn't say anything about you that I wouldn't say to your face. I'm very proud of you, Son."

"Thanks, Dad, but I've still got some ways to go to measure up to you."

"You two are quite a mutual-admiration society, aren't you?" Anna smiled. "It's great to see that you're so close."

Tom smiled back. "Well thanks, but it's natural out here. It's also close to my bedtime." He rose and shook Anna's hand politely, adding "I usually get up before 5:00, so I'm going to wish you a goodnight."

"You are such a gentleman!" she smiled. "I wish you the same."

Anna and Jason remained seated on the broad porch, relaxing in their comfortable chairs. A few minutes passed without a word before Anna broke the silence.

"You haven't offered to show me the skull yet, Jason. Do you mind if I take a look at that, too?" she asked.

Jason paused just a moment, wondering how to explain its sudden disappearance, or the spectre of the mysterious orb. "I hate to admit that it was somehow stolen from my room," he said.

Anna turned to look at him in surprise. "How did you not secure it?" she asked.

Jason swallowed. "I was in the room when it happened. It was dark, the door and windows were closed, but somehow it vanished."

"And you never heard a sound?" Anna asked in disbelief.

"Actually, I saw... something. Something I can't explain," Jason said. "I know this sounds ridiculous, but there was a shape that floated across the room. It looked more or less like a large soap-bubble. All I could see was a slight distortion around the edges, like reflected light."

"And you think this 'shape' had something to do with the missing skull?"

"I have no other explanation," Jason replied, looking evenly back at her. "It was there in plain sight on my dresser, wrapped in a cloth, and then it was gone. The cloth was there, the skull was gone."

There was a long moment of silence before Anna spoke again. "Jason, I am a woman of science. I can't easily accept your explanation."

25

"I understand perfectly, and I can't either" Jason replied. "It's just that I can't...imagine where it went. And I know it sounds strange, but I did see the shape, and when I turned on the light, it was gone."

The two sat in a slightly-awkward silence for another minute or two, watching the crescent sliver of moon sink toward the horizon in the inky darkness as thousands of stars emerged. At last Anna spoke.

"Jason, I'm going to share something with you that I haven't ever told anyone. I say this only because of this circumstance. I have seen something I couldn't explain, too. One night," she continued, "I was camped near Mesa Verde. I had been helping document a Puebloan-culture dwelling. Their first civilization disappeared rather abruptly, as you know, and most of what we know about them comes from the amazing cliff dwellings they left behind. That night, I was lying awake, just marveling at the stars, and I saw some of them seem to ripple. They moved slightly. As I watched, I realized there was a shape moving between me and them. It was...almost invisible, but somehow seemed transparent. It passed slowly across the sky, and I couldn't tell if it was close and small, or huge, and far away. Because I had no idea what I had seen, and didn't want to seem crazy, I never told anyone else about it. Until now."

Jason stared at her for a long moment. "Then you believe me?" he asked.

"I guess I'm just saying that I don't disbelieve you. It's possible that you and I saw much the same phenomena."

"But it took the skull!" Jason asserted.

"If that's true, then I don't know exactly what it is we are dealing with."

"Professor Thompson, there's more that I haven't told you. I don't want you to think I've lost my mind, but I have seen a couple of other things that have me on edge. I can't fit the pieces together, and they may not be connected at all..."

"Please tell me everything, Jason. Maybe together we can sort them out."

Jason proceeded to relate the story of the unusual den, and the strange marks he saw there. When he added the story of the shaft he had discovered, Anna was completely hooked.

"Can you take me to these places in the morning?" she asked.

"We can be there at first light. Plan to ride at 6:00," he told her. "There's a good path most of the way and we can ride in the dark. It will be light before we get there. I'll pack some extra gear we might need."

"I'll be looking forward to it," Anna said. "I guess we should both be getting some sleep, then."

Jason rose and faced her. "Goodnight, Professor," Jason said, with a slight bow of his head.

"Please, call me Anna," she laughed. 'Professor' is much too formal!" Anna laughed. "Just treat me like family."

Jason smiled at her. "Well then, goodnight, Anna!" he said. "I'll see you in the morning."

•

As promised, the pair were saddled up and on the trail in darkness. They watched the sun's glow spread behind the eastern mountains as they rode. A few clouds reflected a soft pink light on the range and the stirring cattle. The chill air carried the scent of hay, cattle, and leather. Overhead a hawk soared in lazy loops.

"You live in a world of enchantment here," Anna said as they ambled slowly along.

"You're right," Jason replied. "Sometimes when a place becomes too familiar you can begin to overlook the beauty. Being away from it for a while has helped me appreciate it more."

They reached the cliff face and followed Jason's earlier path, soon locating the bones. They then back-tracked to where he had found the den.

"The tracks were inside, so we can probably still find them," Jason said, stepping carefully toward the opening, only to be hit with a repulsive smell.

"Oh gag!" he said, stepping back. "It's not all enchantment! I think there must be a skunk in there." He walked back to his pack and pulled out a portable spotlight. Two million candlepower flooded the interior of the hole. Sure enough, against the back wall a skunk was huddled. The opening was just within its range.

Anna wasn't to be denied. "Hold that light low for contrast, and let me get a photo," she said. She brought out her camera, held her nose, and reached inside, hitting the shutter on motor-drive as she steadily turned it.

The pair retreated rapidly, leaving the anxious skunk alone. After walking their horses a hundred feet upwind, Anna pulled her camera back out to see the images. Most of the tracks Jason had seen before were gone. He mentally kicked himself for not having photographed the strange prints when he first saw them, but recalled the sudden fear that had driven him from the hole.

Anna was still paging through the photos, and at last spoke. "Well, I've got something on a few. It's an oblique angle, not straight down, and it may have been disturbed by that skunk or some other animal, but I can see at least a partial mark like you described. The question I have is, how do you know that wasn't made by someone poking a stick into the ground?"

"There were three of them, evenly spaced about a foot apart. The center one was offset from the other two, like footprints usually are. I can't swear to it, of course, because I've never seen marks like them, and there were only three." He quickly stooped and smoothed a patch of sand, roughly reproducing what he had seen before, small circles radiating around a roundish central depression. "Rather like that."

Anna studied his marks, and then her phone. "Well, I can see about half of one track, but it is very much as you draw it. I believe you saw it as you say."

"Thanks, it's good to know I'm not the only one," he told her.

"Jason," she began, "I know you are majoring in forensic anthropology, and have taken mostly lab classes, so you don't have much training yet in field work. I want you to remember this much, as we do in paleontology or archaeology. Document everything note-worthy you come across, *in situ*, before you touch anything. Measure and preserve every dimension and aspect possible. Take photos with something for perspective. Photograph the surroundings. It'll make your teachers much happier."

28

Jason took her lecture in stride. He admitted that he hadn't made a very scientific approach and agreed that he would try to follow her recommendations. He was glad, though, that she had at least gained a shred of evidence that supported what he had told her. Maybe it was time for the rest. "Do you think you might be up to a climb? I could show you that tunnel if you like."

"Of course!" Anna replied brightly. "I came all this way to help solve a mystery. So far all I have is stories, and photos. I could have had that from the university. Lead on!"

When they got to the foot of the cleft that concealed the tunnel, Jason pulled out a pack. Inside, he told her, he had a thousand feet of light cord, and a hundred feet of extra rope, in case they had trouble during the climb. The cord could be used to measure the depth of the tunnel. He had also packed extra water. He tossed his floodlight on top. Hefting it over his shoulders, he realized that the extra weight would make the climb more difficult.

Leaving the horses, it took the pair half an hour to scramble up the steep talus slope, and another twenty minutes to scale the cliff. Jason, climbing ahead with the rope from his pack, had quickly set two solid cams, looped the rope through, and dropped it to Anna, who tied on the pack. After hauling it up, he dropped it back down, giving her an extra measure of safety as she scaled the slickrock face.

At the opening of the tunnel Jason tied the cord to another cam at the entrance. Remembering the empty interior, he also scooped up a handful of small stones and put them in his pocket. They might come in handy, too, he thought.

Slowly they began to walk the length of the corridor, playing out the cord behind them. Using only a small flashlight with a red lens cover, they conserved both the powerful beam of the floodlight and their own night vision. In ten minutes they had reached the end of their thousand feet of cord. Jason stopped long enough to weight the end with a small stone, and they moved forward, carefully counting their steps. Another two hundred feet brought them to a halt. There, just as he had described, Anna saw the looming blackness that swallowed their feeble light.

Saying not a word, Jason set down his pack and removed the floodlight. When he clicked it on, their eyes were overwhelmed for a moment before adjusting to the sweep of the beam across the polished surface of the sandstone. The opposite wall was visible sixty feet away, faint layers of color streaking its surface. Jason aimed the light up, and they craned their necks to see the beam swallowed by the distance. Reversing the light brought a similar result. The lower wall faded from view in a few hundred feet. The bottom of the shaft must be lower than the level of the ranch house, he realized with a start.

Afraid to raise his voice in the cathedral-like silence, Jason whispered. "Should I drop a stone?" he asked. He realized that he had neglected to tell Anna of the strange reaction he had gotten to his earlier attempt to determine the depth of the hole.

"Sure, go ahead," she replied, and Jason pulled not one, but three walnut-sized stones from his pocket, and tossed them into the abyss. A faint, long delayed clink, followed a moment later by an almost imperceptible clatter, gave them a sense of the depth of the shaft. "Almost ten seconds," Anna whispered. "That's about another five hundred feet or more to the bottom. And only one pebble skipped off something, so it may be perfectly vertical the entire way."

The two pondered in silence for a moment, listening. Jason was especially alert, having heard, or at least sensed, something moving down there before. This time, however, there was not a hint of sound. "I think we've seen all we can, let's get out of here," Anna said, and Jason nodded his agreement.

•

That night the weather changed abruptly, and thunder rumbled as lightning illuminated the house in dramatic flashes. Rain poured down from the plateau above, filling the dry washes across the ranches and roads below. The sun was just beginning to send shafts of light through the dark overcast by 8:00 in the morning as Juanita rolled out a cart piled high with eggs, biscuits, ham, orange juice and coffee.

"Thanks, Juanita," Tom said. "You've cooked enough for a small army, why don't you take a break and join us. I'm sure Anna would appreciate some feminine company instead of just rough cowboys to talk to." Both

Anna and Juanita laughed aloud at that announcement, but Juanita accepted the offer, and joined them at the table.

"I peeked out the back of the house this morning," Jason announced. "There's fresh snow up on the plateau, but just at the top. We're still four degrees above freezing here, so this drizzle should be ending soon, no snow for us."

"That's good news, then," Tom replied. "No sense in stressing the new calves any more than they are. Looks like we're in for a couple of colder days, though. We're always glad for the rain," he told Anna. "If it wasn't for the occasional storm, the springs along the foot of the cliffs, and irrigation from the creek, we couldn't even run cattle here. It's almost as dry as a desert."

"That's not a problem right now, anyway," Jason added. "I'm glad that you don't have to leave today, Anna, because there's probably about three feet of water over the road out. It's mostly standing water there, so the road should be passable once it drains off."

Anna smiled at them. "I really don't have to be back at school in a hurry, so I'm happy to accept your hospitality for another day or two," she said. "Besides, I haven't quite gotten to the bottom of your little local mystery. We didn't get a chance to talk about it last night, Tom, but I have a question for you. Are you aware of any sort of government project that ever took place up on the plateau? Maybe a military operation?"

"No," Tom replied. "That really doesn't mean much, though, because it's almost a different world up there. Nobody lives on top since there's no water. It's just rocks and sand, and a few trees."

"If either one of you feel up to a drive, I'd like to look around on the plateau," Anna said as they finished their breakfast. "I don't really want to go alone, though."

"I'd be happy to go, Anna," Jason volunteered. "I think we'd better take my truck, though. It's got all-wheel drive and will handle off-road better than your car. And if we take the jeep trail up the range, we can avoid that flood. Want to go today?"

"That's what I was hoping you'd say, Jason. Yes, I really do. I don't want to waste the short time I have here. Let's go when you're ready."

"Give me ten minutes and meet me on the porch."

•

The drive up the steep switch-backed track was a challenge, and the truck bounced over boulders and into ruts, but a two-hour drive with Anna studying the map had gotten them close to where she wanted to be. Jason's preparations had included grabbing a set of topographical maps that showed the cliff faces, the ranch, and a large swath of the plateau above. "The maps will surely come in handy," Anna said, "but I thought to take a GPS reading of our location when we were at the entrance to the tunnel. Based on the angle we traveled, I think I can come close to pin-pointing the spot above the shaft. Let's see what we find."

"Anna, I don't want to make this whole thing seem any weirder than it already is," Jason said, "but there's something I think I need to tell you. Another strange thing happened last night during the storm."

"What was that?" Anna asked, surprised.

"Well, the first time I was in the tunnel and made it to the shaft, I tried to judge the depth. I had nothing else to throw down there, so I used a bullet from my 45."

"That was smart, Jason. So why is that strange?"

"This morning, when I got up, I found a bullet on my dresser, right where the skull had been. I never leave bullets lying around, much less on my dresser. I looked it over closely. There are scratches on the brass, and the nose was slightly flattened and scratched. I think it's the same one I threw down there."

If Anna was driving, she would have stopped the truck. Her jaw went slack, and Jason glanced from his driving to see her staring at her hands as if lost in thought. At last she spoke. "Did you see anything?"

"No, nothing but the lightning flashing. The rain was a bit noisy, but I didn't hear anything else, either."

Anna paused a long moment before asking "Do you have that bullet, Jason? Could I see it?"

"Yes, it's right here," he said, and fished it from his shirt pocket. "I didn't want to say anything in front of Dad and Juanita at breakfast, but I wanted you to know."

Anna turned the bullet over in her fingers, examining it as best she could in the bouncing truck. "Jason, there is something very strange going on here, and I'm not even sure that I really want to know what it is."

Jason nodded in agreement. "The way I see it, it was a sort of peace offering," he replied. "I think that whatever we are dealing with is intelligent and wanted to let us know that it wasn't a threat. It returned my property. I think it may have been reclaiming its own when it took the skull."

Anna pondered the suggestion for a moment, and then admitted Jason could be right. "It does make sense...but who, or what could it be? It just leads to a lot more questions. Does it live in that hole? Where is it from? Is it alien, or just some unknown species? And is it just some sort of sphere, or does it really have the teeth and fang that were on that skull? That, most definitely, looked like a carnivore to me!"

"I know. I can't stop thinking about where this is all leading, and if we should be going there alone."

"Well, we can't just call NASA and say, hey, we think we found aliens, and they live in Arizona," Anna said.

"Right, but should we tell anyone else?"

"Jason, right now we don't have enough proof to convince anyone who hasn't at least been to that pit. We need something more tangible."

"Well, maybe we can find it nearby. We are almost to your coordinates," Jason said. "I think we'll have to get out and walk from here."

They hiked over rocky terrain as Anna repeatedly checked their coordinates on her GPS. The dusting of morning snow that had followed the rain, along with the icy temperatures, made the going treacherous. Jason often lent a hand to pull Anna up large boulders that blocked their path, but after a half-mile they called a halt.

"This must be the place, Jason. My GPS says we are right over the shaft. Do you see any sign of it?"

"No, but let me look around," he replied, and began an energetic and exhausting spiral search, each circuit widening around Anna's position. For her part Anna stood on a high boulder and used field glasses to examine each quadrant in detail. At last Jason called out. "Over here, Anna. I think I've found something!"

Anna made her way toward the sound of his voice, and eventually found him standing over a narrow cleft between two boulders.

"What is that?" Anna asked. "Does that lead to the shaft?"

"I don't know, but it's not really the hole that's important. Look around. Do you notice anything unusual?"

Anna cast her eyes around his position. "Not really, just more rocks."

"Stand here and look this way."

Anna did as he asked.

"See the hole here? Now let your eyes follow that line. See the depression in the ground? It curves to the left..."

Ann looked, and sure enough could see a curving line that seemed free of rocks and boulders, almost a clear path.

"Follow me," Jason said, and began to walk and count his paces. As he did, the nearly-stone-free path turned continually to the left. In only little more than a hundred and fifty paces they had arrived back at their starting point.

"It's a cap,: Jason offered. "Like a round lid on a bottle. Whatever dug that shaft, re-covered and camouflaged it. There's no way of knowing how thick this lid is, but I think we're directly above the shaft."

Anna could see the logic of what he said. She re-checked her GPS coordinates and her calculations. "I'm off by about seventy-five feet," she said. "I probably misjudged the angle of your tunnel by a degree or so. This has got to be it."

"So, what do we do now that we've found it?" Jason asked. "Leave a peace offering?"

"Do you think that narrow slot actually connects to the shaft?" she asked. "If so, try dropping your bullet back down there."

"Good idea. It could actually be a place where rain has eroded the cover a bit. Let me see if I can find out." He picked up a long stick and poked it into the slot, gently at first, and then a bit more forcefully. It suddenly broke through, and he almost dropped it. "Looks like it passes through into some sort of deeper opening, for sure."

"Try it, Jason. It's just a bullet, and it doesn't offer any proof of anything to anyone but you, and me, I guess..."

Jason took the bullet back out of his shirt pocket and gave it a sharp pitch into the depth of the slot. "I guess if it comes back tomorrow, we'll know more. About what, though, I have no idea!"

"Ok, I guess we've done all we can here," Anna said. "We know there's a cap at the place it was bored, and we have the coordinates exactly now. Let's head home."

The tough hike back to their truck took another half hour, by which time the sky had cleared, and the sun shone down from a bowl of blue sky. The truck sat in bright sunshine, which made the shock of its appearance more devastating. Part of a rear quarter-panel had been cut away, and there were deep cuts on both sides. Jason pulled out his gun and approached it with caution, keeping Anna close behind him.

Large scratches surrounded the broken passenger window. He cautiously approached and peeked inside. The truck was empty, but he realized with a start that the seats were in shreds, and part of the dashboard had been torn out. No, he realized as he looked closer. It had been cut away, too.

Making sure there was nothing of danger still in the truck, they quickly climbed in and started it up. Thankfully it ran. It took Jason a minute to get it turned around, and they started back the direction they had come as fast as was safe. Anna sat close to him, or as far from the broken window as decorum would allow. As he drove, she examined the deep cuts in the dashboard and seat.

"This one slices all the way through the vinyl in a straight line, and this one looks like it cut into the steel," she said. "Whoever did this had to use a power tool. I wonder why they didn't just disable the truck."

"Maybe they didn't want us to stay around, and thought they'd scare us off," Jason replied. "Or maybe," he paused, "they didn't really understand trucks, and just wanted to kill it."

Anna fell silent. If it was an animal of some sort that did this, she wouldn't want to meet it. This wasn't the work of the friendly entity she had pictured only minutes earlier.

Chapter Five

"SO, DID YOU TWO FIND anything interesting up there on the plateau today? You missed lunch, so you must be hungry." Tom said as they walked wearily into the house. The afternoon was half gone, but food was the farthest thing from either of their minds.

"Dad, I've got some bad news. I'm going to need a new truck," Tom replied.

"Oh no, are you two OK? You had some sort of accident up there?"

"We're both fine, no injuries, but I think you should step outside for a moment," Jason replied.

Tom followed him out the door, with Anna close behind. Tom got a worried look as he saw the outside of the truck. "You were attacked by a bear?" he asked.

"Dad, it's worse than that, but please don't tell anyone what I'm about to tell you. Take a look at this," he said, and opened the door to expose the deep, straight cut into the steel frame. "There's others just like it. Remember the clean cut through the cattle we found? How they were practically dissected? This might have been the same tool. It happened while we were hiking. We had left it for about ninety minutes."

"Some fool up there is stealing our cattle, then, and doesn't like you nosing around," Tom said.

"I wish that was all it was, Dad. There's a lot more to the story," Jason said. He lowered the tailgate of the truck, and the three of them sat there in the late afternoon sun as he came clean about everything that had happened. Anna chimed in to verify the details of the afternoon, the tunnel, and the shaft.

"You saw that skull yourself, Dad. I didn't make that up. That creature was completely unknown."

"I only saw the photos, Tom," Anna added, "but I can verify that it was nothing known to science. That's why I came here in the first place."

"So, you really saw this...sphere...float across your room, and then the skull was gone?" Tom asked.

"Dad, I would never make up such a thing. I only know that I saw something move, but it didn't appear solid, or at least, I think I could see *through* it. The next morning the skull was gone."

There was a pause, and Jason could almost hear Tom's brain grinding away at the question. At last he spoke. "OK, so now you've given it the bullet back, and been attacked, or at least your truck was. What do you make of that behavior, if this thing exists? It doesn't make sense."

"I know, Dad. That's why we need your help now. I don't know what to do next. Is it a threat? If so, can we rightfully keep it a secret?"

"We can't even swear that it's an 'it' at this point, Jason. It could be a man with a power tool. And if he's living up on the plateau, he's not likely to come down here looking for trouble. Food, sure, I could understand that. But not a fight. He's got everything to lose, nothing to gain."

At this point Anna could wait no longer. "There are a couple of other things to consider here. The first is that I took a closer look after Jason parked the truck. The bed frame was cut several inches deep, and the dashboard was cut away."

"Right, we all saw that," Jason said. "Somebody used a power-tool while we were away."

"We didn't go terribly far from the truck," Anna said. "Why didn't we hear anything?"

Jason paused. "You're right, it would have taken a big, noisy saw to cut metal,' he admitted. "So how did it get cut up?"

"The steel wasn't cut," Anna said.

"But we can all see the damage," Tom said.

"Oh, it's damaged alright, but it's not cut by any power tool," Anna told him. "It was melted."

"Melted?" Tom said. "Wouldn't that take a laser?"

"Yes, and a lot of energy," Anna replied. "Not something the wild man of the mountain is likely to have lying around. Also, I have another theory. I think we may be dealing with more than one entity."

"You mean..." Jason started.

"Yes, I do. There are two distinct sets of motivations at work here, and unless we have met a schizophrenic alien..."

The men sat in silence again for a second, pondering this new idea. At length Tom spoke again. "So, if there are two, and one is hostile, or at least potentially dangerous, and the other seems benign, what's going on, and how do we respond?"

"The good one, or at least the one that has seemed to send us a message, might be willing to communicate further if we give it a chance," Jason offered. "It might even return the bullet a second time. Wouldn't that be a sign?"

"Tell you what," Tom said. "I have a game camera, the sort that uses infra-red wavelength to take photos of moving heat sources. We could set it up in your room and see if it captures anything."

"Great idea, Dad!" Jason said.

"I agree," said Anna. "It's a start. Maybe we can learn something about it. Let's just hope it's motivated to return."

·

Jason could barely sleep that night but stayed in his own room for fear that any change could make the visitor cautious. It hadn't been afraid of him before, and he really didn't think it would be dangerous now. Nevertheless, for the first time in his life he slept with his revolver on the night-stand. Tom gave Anna a gun as well, a small pistol that would at least attract their attention if it was used in the night. Tom did much the same, and all three retired at a reasonable hour, only to lie awake listening to the sounds of the night.

After two long hours fatigue finally overtook Jason, and he slept fitfully. Dreams of trying to run from some danger but being stuck in mud disturbed his rest. He was finally sleeping well when he thought he'd heard a sound in the room. Without moving he opened his eyes but could see nothing. Very slowly he rolled to his right, so he could see toward the windows. At first, he again saw nothing, then a glimmer of light appeared and seemed to grow steadily brighter. He stared at it, trying to make out a shape behind it. It increased in intensity until it was almost dazzling, at which point he suddenly called out. "Dad, Anna, there's something here!" Within a second the light faded and disappeared.

"I'm on my way!" Tom's answering shout echoed down the hallway.

By the time his father arrived in the room, Jason had the lights on, and was removing the disc from the camera. "Quick, let's see if we got anything," he said as Anna stepped into the room, wrapped in a heavy bathrobe, and looking half awake.

"What happened? Are you OK? Did you see something?" she asked.

"Oh, yeah," Jason said, "and I hope we have some evidence now that it's really trying to...trying to..." He paused a moment before exclaiming "I know what it's trying to do! It is trying to communicate with us, and it just did! It told me something!"

"What? What are you saying? It spoke to you?" Anna demanded.

"No, not exactly spoke..." Jason was suddenly calm. "It just somehow…told me things. There was a bright light, and now...I seem to understand some things about it."

"I've got the disc open," Tom said from the computer. "Let's see if we got anything here..." He scanned through a row of seemingly blank images before one suddenly had substance.

Tom studied the photos closely. "It's not very clear, but I can definitely see something there. It looks like a sphere alright, just as Jason said," Tom pointed out. "It's shining on one side. The surface is just a slight distortion of the background, but with a little imagination it almost looks like it's made of metal to me," he added. "Like silver, or even mercury. There seem to be ripples in the image, like a thick liquid..."

Anna was leaning over his shoulder and pointing excitedly at the photo. "It seems to be transparent, as Jason said, or a hi-definition display!"

"Look at this one," Tom said, paging through the images. "It's shining a light, directly at Jason."

"What was that light, Jason?" Anna asked. "Is that the form of communication? Did it tell you anything?"

"I can't say, exactly, that it said any one thing. It's like it wanted to tell me about itself, about what it's doing here. I got the distinct feeling that it wasn't a threat, and that it wanted to offer help. I shouldn't have shouted. I have a feeling there was much more, and I startled it away."

"The question I have is…" Anna said, "could it harbor some small life form, or is it just a machine?"

Jason was certain now that the sphere wasn't a life form at all. "It made itself clear that it's just a communication device, a messenger," he said. "It's a robot, put here to perform tasks, like..." He suddenly jumped up and ran to his dresser. There, back in its place, was the bullet, a bit more battered than before.

Anna gasped, and sank into the bedroom chair.

Tom scratched his head, looking somehow amused. "Well, now I've seen it all," he said.

"It's pretty amazing," Jason agreed. "I'm just glad that now, with the photos, you can see that it wasn't just my imagination. I really did see something, or at least the outline of something."

"I have a theory about why it's invisible," Anna said. "It's obviously not just a hollow bubble, or it couldn't have taken the skull, or brought the bullet back. I think it uses some sort of masking technology. From the photos, it almost looks like it's projecting the view of whatever's on the opposite side, in 360 degrees. It's sort of filling in the hole it creates in the image seen by each viewer. Does that make sense?"

"Yes!" Jason said. "Now that you describe it that way, that's exactly what it looks like. The distortion I saw was probably just a flaw in the way it portrays things. I could see my wall and window, not really through it, but projected on the surface. Maybe from the interior?"

"Possibly, or more likely a form of liquid crystal display, maybe something more advanced," Anna said.

"If it's really a solid, and not just a bubble, how does it fly?" Tom asked. "It didn't seem to have any sort of propulsion system, and it makes no noise."

"I'm guessing again, but maybe it's a form of magnetic levitation," Anna answered. "It could be using the Earth's magnetic field to fly, resisting like two positive magnetic poles push each other away."

"Incredible," Tom said. "To think that something like that can be done, and we're still using helicopters when we could just hover."

"But it didn't tell me what it's doing here," Jason said. "What could it want?"

"This is a bit beyond my expertise, Jason…" Anna started, "and I'm not sure I can tell you anything you don't already sense."

"Well, it seems like it really is trying to do some sort of service to someone, "Tom said, "and it sure doesn't seem hostile."

"But that still leaves us with the challenge of the crazy…whatever it is, with the laser," Anna replied. "What do you suppose that's about, Jason? Did it say?"

"No, but I think it wanted to," Jason answered. "I had the sense that it was trying to, not threaten me, but warn me somehow. I only hope it will come back."

"How do you think it even got in here?" Tom asked. "The windows and doors are closed."

"If it's been sent by some really-advanced civilization," Anna began slowly, "it's possible that they have learned to pass objects through each other. I know it sounds unbelievable, but it's scientifically conceivable on an atomic level. As an example, you've probably seen photographs of entire galaxies, with more than a billion stars, so many they look like solid objects?"

"Sure," Jason said. "Lots of those, especially in the Hubble photographs."

"Have you ever seen photos of two galaxies colliding?" Anna asked.

"Yes, two at right angles, passing through each other," Jason answered.

"Well, when two galaxies do that, the stars don't even collide," Anna said. "The spaces between them are so vast that they pass right through each other. Gravity interacts, but little else. On an atomic level, all matter is mostly space. Neutrinos are atomic particles so small they go right through us all the time, and they don't hit anything. Billions of them are constantly passing through the entire earth that way without ever striking another particle."

Tom stood silently contemplating what he had heard. At last he spoke. "So, you think we are dealing with an intelligence that has mastered space in a way we can barely imagine?"

"That's what it seems," Anna answered.

No one slept the rest of the night as they discussed and debated what they had seen.

It was almost dawn when the three returned to their rooms, the excitement and adrenaline finally fading. That brief repose was ended an hour later by a phone call. Juanita had arrived and was knocking on Jason's door. "There's a telephone call for you, Jason. It's Mrs. Martin. Seems something has happened at her ranch."

Jason sprang from his bed and hurried to take the landline call, kicking himself for never having offered Ashley his cell number. "Yes, Ashley? Is everything OK?" he asked.

"Jason, you may want to come over when you get a chance. The men found another cow slaughtered this morning. Or, at least part of one."

"I'll be there in fifteen minutes!" he said, then dashed through the house shouting for Tom and Anna.

•

They made the drive to the Circle M in record time, Tom's truck splashing through the foot of standing water that remained in one of the washes. They crunched across the gravel of the front yard and met Ashley coming down the steps. "It was just a little way from here, around back of the barn," she told them, and they hurried to follow her.

The scene wasn't pretty. Her two hired hands, Chuck and Mosely, were poking around the butchered remains of the cow, still steaming in the chill morning air. There wasn't much left of the poor animal. Whatever had killed it had sliced it up neatly and made off with most of it. The area was splattered with blood, but the gravel that covered it effectively concealed any readable tracks.

"It's hard to believe that someone could do this so close to the barn. That takes nerve!" Tom commented.

"It weren't no 'someone,'" said Chuck. "This is something spooky. You don't have to take my word for it. You can ask Mosely."

Everyone turned toward Mosely, widely considered the best cowhand in the area. At 60 years old, he had seen it all, and done it all, everyone said. Mosely scanned the faces staring at him a moment before speaking.

"You know, I was born back east, got treated bad just 'cause I was black," he said. "I've been living on ranches, here and in Colorado, for more than 45 years. I've always been treated well here. People take me as a man, for what I know, and do, and how I handle myself. I've always told the truth. You've been real good to me, and I'm gonna' miss working for you, Miss Martin, but I've gotta go."

"Wait! Please wait just a moment, Mosely," Ashley said, as the rest stood dumbfounded. "You can't just walk away without telling me why."

"That thing I saw wasn't human," Moseley said, "and it weren't an animal, either, that's why. If it can do that to a cow, what would'a been left of me if I had come across it a minute sooner?"

"Please, Mosely, tell me what you saw!" Ashley said.

Mosely stood silently for a moment, and ran his weathered hand across his brow, as if wiping off imaginary sweat. In that moment, no one noticed the chill of the morning.

"I didn't see it real clear, 'cause it wasn't daylight yet," Mosely said at last, "just stars and the glow of the dawn starting. I thought I heard something and came out of the barn there. At first, I just saw a shadow. It was big, I can tell you that. I thought it was a bear, and started to run for my gun, to go protect the horses."

"What else did you see, Mosely?" Tom asked. "How do you know it wasn't a bear?"

"It made a sound, not a growl, exactly, but an ugly sort of scream. It didn't sound like anything a bear does," Mosely said. "When it stood up, I could see it was bigger than any bear. Then it just walked off with a thousand pounds of beef like it was nothing. A bear can't do that, either. I watched it disappear through that wash over there," he pointed, "heading toward the cliffs. It was really tall, and it seemed like it turned to look at me just before it disappeared. It was still dark, but I think I could see a mouth full of teeth, on top... No, ma'am, I'm awful sorry, but I think I'll be moving on, and find another ranch to work. I wish you all well. Be safe," he said, and turned back toward the small bunkhouse that had been his home for fifteen years.

The group stood watching him walk away. No one spoke. Chuck looked shaken, and Ashley was pale. Jason glanced at Anna, who was already looking his way. Tom seemed at a loss for words. At last Jason spoke. "Dad, why don't you get Ashley and Anna back in the house, fix some coffee to warm them up. I'll be in in a couple of minutes, I'm going to look around."

Jason's suggestion was accepted without a word, and Tom had an arm around them both before they had walked ten feet, each of the women ready to find a sense of security after what they had just witnessed. Jason turned to Chuck. "Want to take a little walk?"

"Sure," Chuck said, and patted his own holster.

Together the two ranchers walked in the direction Mosely had indicated. They passed away from the barns and headed slowly off across the ranch. It wasn't difficult to follow the trail of blood that spattered the ground. As they walked that trail got a bit sparser, but soon they were beyond the gravel, and began to see marks in the rain-softened earth.

"Those could be tracks," Chuck pointed out, "but they sure don't look like anything I recognize."

Jason glanced down at the roughly-circular marks that seemed to create a dense pattern in the ground. Each was broader than the span of his outstretched hand. He didn't like the implications of that. They followed another few hundred feet, until the tracks disappeared across a large expanse of exposed slickrock.

"Let's head back," Jason said. "We're going to need some horses," he said. 'And shotguns,' he thought to himself.

Back at the house, Jason found the others sitting in the living room, cautiously discussing what they had seen. It was apparent in a minute or two that Anna and Tom were avoiding telling Ashley everything they knew. He realized that the three of them needed a conference.

"Chuck and I followed the trail for a ways, but he's going to saddle some horses. It's hard to tell how far that thing ran."

"Better saddle one for me, too," Tom said. "I'm coming along. Anna, would you mind staying here to keep Ashley company for a while?"

Ashley spoke immediately. "Thank you, Tom, but I will be alright, you do what you think is best."

Anna smiled. "I might prefer to stay here with you, if you don't mind," she said.

"Of course, I understand, Anna, thank you," Ashley told her. "Company would be welcome."

"I'll be right back in, Ashley," Anna said. "There's something I want to check on that cow first."

"Of course, take your time. I'll put on another pot of coffee."

Anna followed Tom and Jason back to the barn and the remains of the butchered cow. She paused a moment at the gruesome scene. Kneeling, she examined the cuts. "Just as before, like they were done by a surgeon," she said as she stood.

"Listen," Jason said. "We need to decide together how much we can share, and who we should share it with."

Tom nodded and looked at Anna. She glanced down, and then spoke. "It's important that we don't start a panic, or any wild rumors that could go spreading all over the southwest. If you go hunting this thing, I think we need to tell Chuck something of what it is we might be up against. Tell him it's an unknown kind of animal that I'm here to study. He can already see that it's dangerous. Don't mention the rest. It's too much."

"There's something else you need to know, Anna," Jason said.

"Oh, no. Not again!" she responded. "What new surprise are you going to spring on me?"

Jason cleared his throat. "There's more than one. I think they're breeding."

"What? How can you know this?" she demanded.

"The tracks Chuck and I just saw were obscured so he likely couldn't tell what he was seeing. I could make them out, mostly because I'd seen them clearer before. These were four times the size of the tracks I saw in the den. That one must have been a baby."

Tom and Anna stood in silence for a moment as they sorted through this new information. It made sense, Anna realized. If they were breeding, a growing population would need more food than before. Maybe that's why they were coming down to prey on the cattle and becoming far more brazen.

At that moment, Chuck came around the corner of the barn, leading a pair of saddled horses. Right behind him came Mosely, leading another pair.

"I thought you were leaving, Mosely," Tom said.

"I might be, but I reckon I can't run out on my friends," he replied. "I can't leave unfinished business. Let's see if we can catch up to this critter first."

47

The four were quickly saddled up, and Jason noted with satisfaction that each of them had a scabbard with a shotgun or rifle, in addition to their side-arms. Anna waved them off and headed back to the house.

The four cattlemen made a brief gallop back to the expanse of slickrock where Jason and Chuck had lost the trail, and then spread out, keeping each other within eyesight, casting about for any traces in the warming sun.

"I've got something over here," Mosely called, and they gathered where a smear of blood indicated that perhaps a load had been dropped or set down for a moment. Already there were flies gathering. Based on the direction of travel, they continued toward the plateau, spotting occasional drops of blood but few clear tracks.

At length they came to the foot of the talus slope, and scanned the cliff faces over their heads for any sign. Jason was the first to speak. "There, about half-way up, I think I see something moving."

All four focused on the place Jason indicated by pointing. "Good eyes. That's got to be a big-horn sheep," Chuck opined. "Nothing else can move around on that slickrock."

Mosely reached into his saddlebag and drew out a compact pair of field glasses, aiming toward the moving shape. After a long moment he spoke. "That could be what I saw before," he said. "It's a good thousand feet up there, but it's got that same, yellowish color. And I'll tell you something else. From here, it looks like a spider." He passed the glasses to Tom.

The four sat in silence watching the distant shape scuttle higher up the face of the cliff, moving almost effortlessly.

Chapter Six

A N HOUR LATER ANNA, JASON, AND TOM were sitting with Ashley in her living room, sipping warming coffees, and discussing the morning's events. Ashley was shaken, and they tried to calm her.

"I can't keep losing cattle to that thing, whatever it is," Ashely said firmly. I've got to fight it."

"We're going to get to the bottom of this mystery and put a stop to it," Jason assured her.

Tom explained to Ashley that they had tracked the marauder as far as the cliffs but left out the details of its scuttling climb up the slickrock. "Now that we know where it's coming from, we'll just set a trap for it," Tom said. "We'll get it."

As they talked, Ashley's shock gradually changed to a sense of indignation. She was more angry than scared, and determined to resist whatever it was that had attacked her ranch. "Richard would have wanted me to stand fast against this...thing, whatever it is, and that's what I'm going to do," she said. "I'm not about to let it destroy what he, and his father, worked so hard to build."

Anna felt a strong sense of guilt for not coming clean with Ashley but didn't know if the truth would make the situation any better. "You just need to take care of your own needs, Ashley," she told her. "You are naturally a bit fragile after all this. Let us take care of this problem for you."

"We have the tools to put a stop to this," Tom said. "We can't have it taking our cattle."

"Yes, that's right," Jason chimed in. "You shouldn't worry about a thing, Ashley. Just focus on your own life. Try to relax. Let us handle this."

Eager to get Ashley's mind off the problems, Tom tried to change the subject. "Why don't you join us for dinner tonight, Ashley?" he asked. "I'll have Juanita prepare something special."

"I was thinking about whipping up something myself instead," Jason chimed in. "Maybe I can give Juanita some time off."

"You cook, too?" Ashley asked with a smile, and Anna seemed surprised as well.

"Well, sure. I learned a bunch of my Mom's recipes from her while I was growing up, and they come in handy at college," Jason said. I share a house with two other guys, and neither of them seem to be able to make a cup of tea. I can't live on fast-food, so if I couldn't cook, I'd probably starve. How does lasagna sound?"

"It sounds wonderful!" Ashley said. "What time should I be there?"

"How about 6:30? That will give me plenty of time to get some sleep first. I, um, stayed up late last night."

"Deal. I'll be looking forward to it," she answered.

•

"Well, you seemed to be quite a hit today," Anna said to Jason, as they rode back toward home. "Chasing away the big bad wolf, and now offering to fix dinner for everyone, too?"

"Let's just hope the big bad wolf stays in its lair for a while," Jason said. "I don't feel like facing that beast any time soon, after what we saw today."

The afternoon passed swiftly. Jason was up in the early afternoon and stayed busy in the kitchen after giving Juanita the day off. Tom and Anna followed their own rest with some serious discussions about their next steps.

"I'd like to set a trap for it," Tom told her. "Have you got any thoughts about that?"

"I think we need to know a bit more about its anatomy," Anna told him. "We may not get more than one chance if it's wily. It may be smarter than we're assuming. It made some ghastly cuts in those bones. They weren't broken or chewed, they were sliced like they were made of cheese. That's very disturbing."

Tom paused for a long moment, his mind a turmoil. It seemed like a strange nightmare. "So, if it's not human, and it's not an animal, and it has some sort of…technology, are you convinced it's an alien?"

"That's still only conjecture at this point," Anna said. "We don't even have any real, physical proof there's anything unusual going on. Our evidence is cut up cows, which any butcher shop could produce, plus your truck, and a dented bullet. If we took those bones to the sheriff, or the military, they would think it was a hoax. We could have manufactured all the evidence ourselves. We've got to be rational. We can't let our imaginations run away completely."

"You're right,' Tom said, "but I won't be surprised if it's more bizarre than we expect."

•

Ashley arrived as a warm sunset glow was filling the valley, and the group enjoyed a delicious dinner, accompanied by a bottle of Chianti. The cork was out of the second bottle as they conversed in the living room afterwards. All were pleased to see Ashley looking better, and agreed that some social support was better than her life alone in the big rambling ranch house at Circle M.

"Why don't you just bring some things and stay with us for a few days, Ashley?" Tom suggested. "I think it will do you some good. You can have the suite at the west end of the house. We could arrange some activities, maybe drive up to Durango one day."

"I don't know, Tom... I appreciate the offer, but..."

"I'll only be here a few more days, Ashley, but I would enjoy your company too," Anna added.

"Well, it is tempting. Let me think about it, if that's alright. I'll let you know tomorrow."

"That's fine, take all the time you want, Ashley," Tom said. "The offer is open-ended."

Jason said nothing, fascinated by everything about Ashley, but respectful of her fragility.

They chatted for another hour and were almost ready to call it a night when Anna suddenly froze. She had no choice but to wave for silence, and point. Everyone turned to see a faint distortion that became an obvious orb as it moved into the center of the room and stopped before them.

"What on earth is that?" Ashley said, "Some sort of toy?"

"No, Ashley," Jason whispered. "I'll explain later. Just watch for the moment."

The orb stopped about ten feet in front of where Jason sat in a large armchair. Ashley and Anna watched from the sofa a few feet away as a faint gleam appeared on its surface. No one spoke as it seemed to focus on Jason, growing steadily in intensity until it filled the room with a glow like a bright full moon. Jason sat transfixed. After a long thirty seconds without movement in the room, the light dimmed, and the orb began to slowly back away. As they watched in amazement, it glided toward the thick adobe wall, and passed into it.

"My god, what was that?" Ashley gasped, almost in a state of shock.

"That, Ashley, is what I think we can call the Messenger," Jason replied. "And now I'm beginning to understand what it's all about."

"I think, after that little display, that we are going to have to let Ashley know everything," Anna said. "There's no reason to try to shelter her any further."

"I agree," said Tom. "And that is all the more reason she should come stay here for the next few days."

Ashley looked at them, stunned. "What do you mean? What else is happening around here, besides that animal killing our cows, and now this...this...'Messenger,' or whatever it is?"

The trio looked at each other, each feeling a bit guilty. At last Jason spoke. "Since I'm the one who has been caught up in the middle of this, and have now gotten each of you entangled, I guess I'm the one who should try to explain." He began at the beginning, describing the skull he found, the lair and footprints, the first visit of the Messenger and the disappearance of the skull. He explained how he had shared the story with Anna, who had rushed from the university to see for herself. The tunnel, the shaft, and even the attack on the truck were laid out as they had happened. Ashley shuddered as he explained how the truck seemed to have been cut with a laser but seemed to take the facts in stride.

"So, it seems we are dealing with something that's quite...alien," she said when he had finished. "Is that Messenger thing alien, too, or some sort of government tracking tool following the alien around?"

"You aren't far wrong, from what I think I've learned," Jason replied. "It's a sort of robotic AI, an Artificial Intelligence. When it shone its light on me, it was almost like it was sending me a stream of information. At first, it's just light, but gradually it begins to make sense to me, like the data is sorting itself so I can read it. Or maybe translating itself from a different language, which seems logical, don't you think?"

"That makes perfect sense to me, Jason," said Anna. "I think you get a 4.0 so far."

Jason smiled, and then continued. "I think it *is* a sort of government monitor, but not from our government. Based upon the impressions it gave me, it was brought here long ago by a small group, a colony if you will, from another civilization. Its original purpose seems to have been as some sort of communication device, perhaps to monitor the movements of the group. I think they may have been, shall we say, independent? Rather like alien vagabonds seeking a home in the wilderness. From what I gather, they came here a long time ago."

"So, they're the ones who built the shaft?" Tom asked.

"Yes, I believe that's correct," Jason answered.

"Then why is the shaft empty? What was its purpose?" Tom pressed him.

"I really don't know the answer to that. Maybe there used to be something in it."

"So why are they attacking our cattle now?" Tom asked.

"They aren't. They aren't here anymore. Maybe they left, or maybe they died out," Jason said. "I think they've been gone for a pretty long time, it's hard for me to tell how long. I don't think their measure of time and ours work the same. Twenty might mean twenty centuries, or twenty million years, for all I know."

"The cliffs aren't that old," Anna said. "Judging by erosion rates, I would have to say that the shaft couldn't have been cut and concealed there more than fifty thousand years."

"Fifty thousand years?!" Ashley said. "That's amazing just to think about!"

"It's more likely they are much newer than that," Anna said. "If I had to guess from my limited geological studies and experience with sandstone, I'd guess more than a few hundred years, but probably not more than a few thousand. Maybe as old as the pyramids."

"So, if you think they left, Jason, what about the thing killing our cattle?" Tom asked. "That's not a colonist?"

"No," Jason replied. "I'm afraid that…that was one of their pets," he said.

The others stared at him in stunned silence for a moment.

"You're telling us that what we are dealing with is the abandoned pet of a long-lost alien colony that has decided to come down and eat our cattle?" Tom asked Jason at last, almost in disbelief.

"I'm afraid that's right. Except that it isn't just an abandoned pet, it's become feral. What was once domesticated is now wild, and it's reverted to its instincts."

"That's not good, is it?" Ashley asked sarcastically.

"No, it's not," Jason replied. "But there's worse."

"Geez, Jason, you're starting to scare me here," Anna said. "What's worse?"

Jason paused to look at her a moment before answering. "It's intelligent. An intelligent species we've never encountered."

"So that gives it an advantage over us?" Tom asked.

"I don't necessarily think it's smarter than us, but smart enough to be very dangerous," Jason said. "They have their own language. They can communicate with each other as easily as we do."

"OK, I hear you saying 'they' and 'them,' like there's more than one," Ashley interjected. "How many of these things did they leave behind when the colony died out, and why are they still here?"

"Because," Jason replied, "they are breeding. I don't know how long their life-spans might be, but they are obviously replicating, and I think they are hunting down here now because there are more of them, and they're depleting the food supply up there."

"That's frightening!" Anna said.

"Another advantage they have is that they can use tools. Complex tools," Jason continued. "Maybe not things they create, but things that were left behind by their former masters. Like the laser, or whatever it is, that they used on the cattle...and my truck." he added.

"You learned all this from that light shining on you?" Ashley asked.

"I can't explain how exactly, but yes, that's essentially correct," Jason told her.

"Let me see if I can summarize what you've explained." Tom said. "They're smart, they have tools or perhaps weapons of some sort that were left over from an advanced civilization. They've reverted to wild animals, they're multiplying, hungry, and they are getting bolder."

"Correct," Jason replied.

"Don't you think we should call the sheriff? Or the army?" Ashley asked.

"How do you think they would react, if they didn't just lock us in a padded cell?" Anna asked. "We have no proof, no real evidence at all, except what we're seen. And if we did succeed in alerting the government, and they determined what was hiding in the cliffs, they'd probably drop a nuclear bomb on the whole place."

"Good point," Tom said. "Maybe we should wait a bit before we try to call in the Marines. Jason, tell me, did your Messenger have any suggestions about what we should do?"

"If I'm interpreting the message correctly, I don't think it said anything more than 'patience.' I think it's intelligent as well, even though it's mechanical. I think part of its duty is to monitor these pets, to care for them somehow. I got the sense that it's trying to resolve things."

"Well, it better act fast," Tom replied, "because if I get a clear shot at one of those beasts, I'm inclined to see what color they bleed. I'm tired of losing cattle."

"This whole thing just keeps sounding worse and worse," Ashley said. "Jason, I just hope you know what you're doing, but I'll give you every bit of support I can, for as long as I can hold out. Then, I think I'm calling for help."

"Thank you, Ashley," Jason replied. "I'm going to try my best not to let you down."

Chapter Seven

DESPITE THEIR FEARS, there were no further incidents with cattle for the rest of the week, and no return of the mysterious orb Jason called the Messenger. Although they rode each day along the bluffs at the foot of the escarpment, there were no fresh tracks, and no evidence of the strange creatures.

"Maybe we scared it off by chasing it," Tom opined, "or maybe the Messenger figured out how to keep it from coming down here."

At week's end, they called an uneasy halt to their efforts. "I've got to return to the university, and so do you, by Tuesday," Anna reminded Jason. "My ex is bringing the kids back Sunday evening, so I can't stall any longer. Plus, I've got a class to teach, and you're in it."

"So true, Professor Thompson" he replied, grinning. "You'll have to tell us about your family sometime. Meanwhile, I'll be looking forward to your lectures."

Convinced the danger had passed for the moment, at least, Ashley returned to her own home, but slept with a gun near her bed. Chuck had urged Mosely to stick around, and he decided that, if kept himself ready, he could face the beast if it returned. They continued to patrol the range and saw the completion of the calving season. Tom did the same, with his own ranch-hands working long hours until every newborn calf was inspected, treated, and branded, and dozens of other jobs handled.

When the semester was ended, Jason couldn't wait to put down the books for a while and spend some time on horseback, enjoying the beauty of the season.

The first week of summer, Anna came to visit after Tom's repeated invitation, and it felt like a reunion of sorts, without the drama that had drawn them all closer together. The party of four got together one day for a drive to a mountain park and a picnic. They marveled at the miles of colorful wildflowers that had sprouted after the big spring rain. Best of all, they had managed to keep their secret, and no other ranches in the area seemed to have been affected.

Jason spent the rest of the summer as a regular ranch hand, mending fences and cutting cows. He was in fine trim, full of muscle and energy. The beginning of the school year was almost hard to face, but he continued to excel in his studies at the university. His biggest surprise came in October when, in a restaurant only blocks from campus, he came upon his father having dinner with Professor Thompson. Anna looked radiant, and Jason escaped unseen. He hadn't expected his father's visit until the following day.

With the approach of Christmas, Tom and Juanita got busy with planning their annual Christmas Eve dinner. The menu would include a turkey stuffed with truffles, a tradition that Isadora had brought with her from Spain, and which Tom insisted on keeping alive. Juanita's expertise would assure the *pavo trufado* would be a success. The family would have more than a dozen guests, including Tom's ranch hands, Ashley and her crew, Juanita's husband and children, couples from two other ranches, and of course, Anna and her children, whom all were eager to meet.

Arriving from the university, Jason hung holiday lights across the porch, found a tree to decorate, and pitched in on the dinner preparations. Despite trying to keep himself busy, though, his mind often wandered to the idea of seeing Ashley again after several months.

At last the big day arrived, and the Cloud home was filled with light and warmth. "Welcome to the C9 Ranch!" Tom told each guest as they arrived at the door. Jason was delighted to meet Anna's two children, Sarah and Michael, who were 18 and 15. Michael was a solid-looking young man, full of energy. Sarah was tall, blonde, and athletic. They were both excited to be spending the holidays on a real, working ranch, and Jason had already promised them a horse-back expedition. Juanita's teens, Luis and Elena, quickly connected with Sarah and Michael, and they were soon answering each other's questions about their schools and lives in very different settings.

Anna arrived for Christmas Eve dinner wearing a beautiful dress that matched the pale green of her eyes, and again seemed to have a glow that Jason had never noted in her classes. She sat to Tom's left, wearing a beautiful diamond pendant, and from his position at the head of the table, Tom raised a toast "to wonderful friends, and bright futures."

After dinner, Jason finally got his chance to spend a few minutes speaking with Ashley after finding her sitting quietly looking out the broad windows. Bright moonlight reflected from snowy peaks many miles in the distance. "I hope everything's going smoothly on your spread," he offered.

"Yes, it is, thanks to Mosely and Chuck over there," she said, nodding toward the two cowboys who were standing near the fireplace with fresh drinks in their hands, talking animatedly with Juanita's husband, Ramiro.

"I'll be around for almost two more weeks, so if you need anything..." Tom began.

"That will be nice," Ashley replied with a coy smile. "I've missed having you a phone call away."

Her every word was a delight to Jason's ears, enchanted as he was by everything about her.

"You know, if you're not busy one day..." he began, shyly, "maybe you could, um, come over for lunch? What's your favorite dish?"

"Ratatouille," she said without hesitation. "Name the day."

"Sure! One day this week, uh, how about Thursday?" he said.

"Sounds great."

After a short silence, Jason spoke. "Ashley, I want you to know that I've missed you too," he said, "It's great to be back."

Ashley just smiled at him, turned away, but glanced back from the corner of her eye. "You know, it's going to be a long winter. It's my first alone, in my entire life. My parents are back east, in Philadelphia, and I've been spending time with them this fall. Maybe I should have stayed there after I got my teaching certificate, but I'd always dreamed of being the frontier school teacher, a little one-room school house on the prairie..."

"You didn't miss that by much here," Jason said. "We only had six students in my senior class!"

"True," she agreed. "It was everything I had wanted, but meeting Richard was like frosting on my dream cake, even though he insisted I give up teaching. He didn't want me to be making that long drive every day."

"I can understand him being protective of you," Jason said. "It's a wild world."

"Living on a ranch, riding horses, it's all like a fantasy for a little girl from the big city," Anna said. "I really didn't miss teaching as much as I feared. But when I lost Richard, I didn't know if I'd lose the dreams, too. But I didn't. I still have dreams, they have just taken different shapes now. Life is funny like that. It leads us to places, and people, that we couldn't imagine from afar..."

"Ashley, I want your dreams to come true, whatever they become," Jason told her. "You are a treasure, and you deserve only the best that life can give you."

"My dreams are closer than you might imagine," she said, and patted his hand.

•

Christmas day dawned bright and sunny, and Jason heard stirrings in the guest wing early. Sarah and Michael were already sitting in the living room when he came down for his first cup of coffee. "Merry Christmas!" he said to them as he entered the room with a steaming mug. "I guess you two are ready to see what's in those packages."

"Sure, but we'll wait until everyone's here," Sarah responded. "Mom's still sleeping. I'm just as excited to be going riding!"

"I guess we'd better do that today," Jason said. "Looks like there might be snow tomorrow."

Moments later Tom came in the door. "I've just been out to the barn. Amazing sunrise this morning!" he said. "Anyone else ready for coffee?"

"I'll have a cup!" Sarah said.

"Ugh, no, thanks, I really don't like it," Michael chimed in. "Got any hot chocolate?"

"I think we can whip some up, pronto, pardner," Tom answered with a grin.

"Sorry, I'm here, I'm awake!" Anna announced as she entered the room. "I didn't mean to hold up the morning."

"Don't worry, Mom, we're not children anymore," Sarah said with a laugh. "We can actually wait a few, calm minutes, before we tear into the gifts like wild animals!"

When the dust had settled, and everyone had enjoyed a hot breakfast courtesy of Jason, Michael and Sarah set their new gifts aside and began talking about the ride they would take. "We'll wait an hour or two," Jason told them. "The day's warming up, but it will still be plenty cold this afternoon. I don't want to take Anna's children, and bring her back popsicles!"

•

Jason led the party of three westward early that afternoon, keeping the sun on their left. Its rays lit the cliffs in a dazzling array of red and yellow hues, which gradually faded as a thin overcast veiled the sky. They rode beyond the western pasture, covering six miles, to where Jason knew of a lone 'hoodoo,' one of the peculiar, eroded columns of rock that marked several places along the Escalante step, and filled the famous Bryce Canyon.

"That is so cool!" Michael said, staring up at the pillar of stone. "I've seen pictures of them before, but never in person. Look at how the layers are colored!"

"What made that?" Sarah asked, and Jason explained how a harder cap rock had protected the sandstone directly below from erosion as the softer stone around it was gradually worn away by rain and freezing.

"It's like it had a hat that protected it," he said.

"That must take a long time," Sarah remarked.

"Thousands of years, I'd guess," Jason replied, "These sand dunes were laid down about forty million years ago, buried, fossilized, and then exposed again by erosion, so what's a few more?"

Dismounting, they walked all around the hoodoo, and Michael pointed out a strange mark, fifteen feet from the ground. "That looks almost like someone wrote something there."

Sure enough, when Jason looked, it appeared that there was something drawn on the side of the stone. "That could be writing from some ancient Indians," Michael offered. "Maybe someone left his mark there, and now erosion has left it higher?"

"Even if it was from a Puebloan culture thousands of years ago this ground at the bottom couldn't have eroded that far," Jason replied, then a thought occurred to him.

"Hey, want to see some real ancient writing?"

"Sure!" they both replied.

"There are some petroglyphs on the slickrock near here. Let's ride on a bit, and I'll show you."

The trio headed northwest following the curving line of the bluffs as Jason searched for the place he had seen the strange markings years before. "It's right around here somewhere," he told them at last. "Look around about twenty feet above the ground."

At last they found their goal, a sheer wall bearing a series of strange marks high above their heads. "How did those get so high?" Michael asked. "Were they really tall?"

"No, but I think they must have used some sort of scaffolding," Jason replied. "Lots of the old hieroglyphics were done far above the ground, for some reason."

As they looked at it, fat snowflakes began to fall around them. With a start, Jason looked up. He had been so focused on their hunt, he had missed the change in the weather. Above, dark clouds had replaced the thin overcast, and a plume of heavy snow was sweeping down the face of the bluff.

"We'd better be heading back. The snow's arriving sooner than they had predicted," Jason told them.

Quickly they turned their horses and began trotting back down the stony trail that had led them to the cliff face. Suddenly Jason heard a cry behind him and turned to see Michael's horse trying to stand after a tumble. He rushed back and found Sarah kneeling over her brother, who was lying in an awkward position, his horse standing next to them. "Are you OK, Michael?" she asked him.

"No, I hurt. I hit my back on that rock," he replied. "The horse just slipped, I think."

"Don't move," Jason said. "If you have a spinal injury, you could make it worse. Try to relax. I'm going to call for help." He quickly had his phone in his hand and hit speed-dial for his dad. "I've got no signal. Do you have yours, Sarah?"

"Mine's showing nothing, too."

The snow had begun falling faster now, already a light dusting was coating Michael's warm jacket, and settling on Sarah's shoulders.

"We've got to move fast," Jason said. "Sarah, do you think you could find your way back to the ranch house alone? I need to stay here with Michael. You need to retrace our steps, keep the cliffs to your left."

"I think I can. I'll try."

"Your horse should know the way, even if you don't," Jason assured her. "Just be careful."

In moments Sarah trotted her horse down the trail, disappearing behind the curve of the slickrock. Jason turned back to Michael. "Can you tell me specifically where the pain is?" he asked, tossing a blanket over him.

"Mostly in the center of my back. It hurts when I breathe."

"OK, just try to lie still. You might have broken a rib when you hit the rock."

"I'm cold," he said.

"Let me see what we can do about that," Jason replied. He removed his fleece-lined jacket and put it over Michael, replacing the blanket after shaking off the gathering snow. Keeping him dry while lying on the ground would be critical to avoiding hypothermia, Jason knew. He went to his horse and retrieved a water-proof poncho and added that to the layers. He wished he could put something under the boy, but it would be impossible without moving him. He dared not.

"I'm going to leave you for a couple of minutes," Jason told him. "I won't be far away, but I'm going to see if I can find any firewood. I won't be out of earshot, so call if you need anything, OK?"

"Sure, Jason. Thanks."

Jason followed the trail as quickly as possible, picking his steps through the rocks, now partially hidden by thickening snow. 'I hope Sarah is getting through quickly,' he thought to himself as he gathered handfuls of dry grass and twigs. A few sticks of dead piñon pine were all the substantial wood he found. Hurrying back, he arranged the dry wood atop the tinder, and struck a match. The flame flickered but held, and he carefully set it under his small heap. A plume of smoke was followed by the satisfying sight of flames jumping, and the comforting incense aroma of the piñon wood. Building a ring of rocks around it, he turned to Michael. "It's not much yet, but I'll get you warmed up soon," he said, before hurrying away to hunt for more wood.

Michael lay awkwardly looking at the flames, wishing that he could get up, but knowing that Jason was doing his best. He tried not to move, but felt a chill spreading through his back. "Jason," he whispered when he had returned, "I feel wet. Am I bleeding?"

Quickly Jason knelt next to Michael. "Where? Is it just snow melting?"

"My back," Michael said. "It stings too. Maybe I'm cut?"

Jason did his best to avoid moving Michael, but all would be in vain if he was slowly bleeding to death. Very carefully he knelt and rolled Michael slightly so that he could see beneath him. A short piece of a stick protruded from his back, and blood had stained a small patch of the ground beneath him, steaming in the cold air. Jason tucked the blanket under his shoulders and hips to try to steady him, then reached to touch the branch. "Does that hurt?" he asked.

"No worse than before," Michael answered.

"You are a very brave guy, Michael," Jason said. "You got poked with a stick. I'm going to try to get that out, so you don't have to lie on it."

"Yes, sir. Thank you." he responded weakly.

Jason carefully pulled on the branch, it fell away, and he tossed it into the fire. He could see that it hadn't gone deep, but it had left a significant wound that needed treatment. He was happy to see that there was no fresh surge of bleeding. Perhaps it was already coagulating. He carefully tucked the edge of the blanket beneath Michael before standing again.

Jason scanned the area around him in the dimming light. The horses seemed fine, but the snow was falling thick and fast, and the wind was steadily rising. He quickly fed more wood onto the dying fire, building the flames higher, and added more rocks to the ring he had built. Then he sat next to Michael, keeping the boy in the center between himself, the fire, and the horses. He hoped help was already on its way.

•

Tom and Anna sat together on the cozy love-seat before the fire, with a clear view of the snow that had begun to fall. Anna fidgeted with her cell phone, then returned to staring out the window.

"I'm sure they would call if there was any sort of trouble, right?" she asked Tom.

"Sure, don't worry, they'll probably ride up any moment. Jason's able to handle 'most anything, and a little snow never bothered him." Inside, however, he was worried. Jason should have had the kids back two hours before, and the thickening clouds had all but obscured the sun, creating an early dusk.

Suddenly, Anna grasped Tom's hand, squeezing tightly. "There," she said. Tom looked in the direction she was facing and saw the merest distortion of the snowflakes outside the window. A moment later the familiar sphere passed through the glass, stopped ten feet in front of them, and began to glow. The light grew and appeared to focus on Anna, swelling in intensity until she almost reached to shield her eyes, but thought better of it. If it was communicating, she wanted to know everything it would tell her. After a moment the light faded, but the object remained, hovering silently in the air before them, now almost invisible.

"What happened, Anna? Did it tell you anything?"

"Yes. Yes, it did, give me a minute to make sense of it all..." She hesitated a moment longer, then said "let's go, we've got to follow it."

Tom was on his feet in an instant and grabbing their coats and hats. "Where are we going, and how are we getting there?" he asked.

"We'd better ride, I don't know if the truck will get us to where they are. They're in trouble."

They rushed to the barn, grateful that the sphere seemed to wait patiently as Tom saddled the horses and scooped up the emergency medical kit he kept there. "Grab those extra horse blankets, too," Anna told him. "We may need them."

Once they were saddled and mounted, the sphere began to emit a faint glow and took off to the west. They spurred their horses across the paddock and through the gate, moving at a gallop. They traveled along the fence-line, following the route they knew Jason would have taken, and had covered nearly two miles when they spotted a shape moving quickly toward them through the snow. "Mom!" Sarah shouted. "Hurry, it's Michael, he's hurt! They're back by the petroglyphs!"

As they rode alongside her, Tom stopped her horse. "Sarah, I want you to ride back to the house and use our phone to call for help. Tell them we rode west from the ranch, and everything you know about where they are. Then, call Ashley. Her number is written on the notepad by the phone. Tell her the same thing. We've got to hurry. This snow is getting thick."

Sarah didn't hesitate a moment but spurred her horse onward toward of the house. Tom and Anna quickly resumed their journey as well, hope and fear mingling in their thoughts.

•

Jason threw his last two sticks onto the dwindling fire and used his gloved hand to quickly lift one of the heated stones to place against Michael, who was occasionally moaning in his sleep. Jason figured that sleep was the one pain-reliever available. The snow was piling up around the pair and their huddled horses, still saddled and ready. Jason wished he had blankets for the horses, too, but had used everything to try to maintain Michael's body temperature. His loss of blood made that even more critical.

Jason rued having started out with the kids when there was a chance of bad weather, even though the snow wasn't predicted to arrive until after nightfall. Now that it was growing dark, it had gotten much heavier. Several inches had accumulated beyond the reach of the fire's modest warmth and the horses stamping feet. It could be hours before help came, and the snow might prevent them from arriving before morning. Lightning flashed above the plateau, putting an exclamation point on his fears. For his own part he had become seriously chilled and was trying hard to avoid hypothermia. Without his coat, his flannel shirt was becoming soaked by the snow, and he resorted to dancing around in place to warm himself. Without a fire, they would both die of exposure.

As the gloom became almost impenetrable darkness with no sign of a rescue party, Jason made another foraging run for firewood. Using his hands, he felt between the rocks and boulders, collecting the scant debris that had gathered there. He returned repeatedly to the fire to toss handfuls of grasses and twigs around it, but the snow had dampened everything. It took almost as much energy to dry the stuff, he thought, as it generated when it burned. It was a zero-sum game. Unless he could find something better to burn, they wouldn't last much longer. He made another effort to find wood, this time heading the opposite direction.

Suddenly out of the darkness he saw a light. "Over here!" he shouted but got no reply. The light moved rapidly his direction, though, and in a moment the Messenger hovered only a few feet from his face. The light shone at him for a couple of seconds only, but he understood. 'Follow,' it had suggested. As it moved away, he followed quickly behind. It led him through the darkness back to camp, and he was surprised to find an old log about three feet long lying next to the fire. He quickly picked it up and began to beat it against a boulder, smashing it into a dozen pieces of various size. These he quickly arranged over the dying embers and sprinkled a bit of the now-dry grass on them. A flame soon flickered, and within minutes a substantial fire had grown, casting a warming circle of light over their crude encampment. Jason turned his back to the fire to dry his shirt, glad for the feeling of warmth that began to reach his skin. He suddenly remembered the Messenger, but there was no sign of it.

An hour later, Jason heard the muffled sound of horses, and used his dying cell phone to cast a light in that direction. Faint as it was, it seemed to have been enough.

"Hello! Over here!" Jason shouted, and was relieved to hear an answering call from his father. A minute later he and Anna picked their way up the faint trail, illuminated by their lights. They immediately wrapped Jason in dry blankets and removed Michael's poncho long enough to add more layers. Jason explained about the stick that had punctured his back, and the loss of blood. Anna checked his vital signs. His pulse was weak but steady, and he was conscious, if drowsy.

"Michael, can you move your toes?" Anna asked, and he responded by doing so. "Good. Don't try to do anything more right now, we still aren't sure if you've hurt your spine. Did you hit that rock when you fell?"

"Yes, and I twisted. It hurt. I didn't feel the stick that Jason found until later."

"OK. We are going to get you out of here and get you to where a doctor can take a look at your back. Just be patient, sweetie."

"Mom..." Michael said. "I love you."

"I love you too, honey. Just hang in there for me."

"Do you think it's safe to move him?" Tom asked when Anna had finished.

"There's a risk, certainly, but we can't leave him on the ground, either," Anna said. "Jason has a blanket pushed about halfway under him. I'm going to try to pull it carefully and try to make a sling of it. Then we can try to lift him."

"But then what?" Tom asked. "We can't put him on a horse."

Just then they both heard a distant roar and turned to listen. It grew rapidly louder, and a minute later a snowcat roared around the bluff a short distance away. Jason was already shining one of the lights, and with its heavy treads it quickly navigated between the boulders to stop only a few yards away. They ran to meet it, and found Ashley and Sarah climbing from the cab.

"I've got a trailer attached," Ashley told them. "I brought two sleeping bags for a mattress, and a stack of blankets. They are sending an ambulance as far as your ranch. Can we lift him?"

"Thank goodness you came," Anna said. "Yes, I think we can, if we each take an edge of the blanket, and walk him over here carefully."

Together the five of them accomplished the task with a minimum of jostling, and soon had Michael bundled securely. "Warm enough now?" Anna asked him.

"Yes, thanks, Mom" he told her. "Don't worry, I'm going to be OK, just come see me."

"Michael, honey, I'll be with you every step of the way."

With Ashley back behind the wheel, Anna climbed into the trailer beside her son, and they headed for the house, leaving Tom and Jason to handle the string of horses. They were mounted in minutes and set off through the snow, now several inches deep.

Riding was difficult in the darkness, and without the advantage of landmarks they followed the track left by the snowcat. It had cut through the snow nearly to bare earth, making their progress easier. The falling snow blanketed a landscape of rocks, sand sage, and rabbit bush, creating strange shapes that seemed to rise before them. Once the sound of the snowcat faded in the distance, the snow seemed to muffle any sound.

Several times they had turned on a light to make their way through the washes, making certain the horses had secure paths on the slopes, but the glare from the snow nearly blinded them, so for the most part they rode in darkness.

"How did you find us so quickly?" Jason asked his father as they rode. "I really thought it would take longer for Sarah to reach you, and for you to find us in the dark."

"We had help," Tom replied. "Your 'Messenger' came to us and communicated with Anna. It led us to you. We were already a couple of miles up the trail when we met Sarah coming down."

Jason didn't respond for a moment, thinking about the series of events. "It came to me, too, Dad. It brought me firewood."

"For an artificial intelligence, that thing's damned smart," Tom said. "It's kind of handy having a life-saving robot zipping around."

"Funny that it showed up just when we needed it, after almost a year," Jason said.

"Yeah, it is. I wonder if it's been watching us the whole time?"

"That's kind of creepy, I guess, when you think about it. Like 'big brother' is watching."

"Well, right now, I'm sure glad it is!" Tom said.

They rode along in silence for a few more minutes before Jason suddenly paused and shone his light on the ground nearby. "What do you make of that, Dad?"

Tom looked to where Jason's light was illuminating dozens of dark spots. Jason walked his horse that direction and shone the light down. "Dad, I think you need to see this."

Tom rode alongside Jason, and immediately felt a chill. The snow was liberally cut by broad, circular depressions nearly a foot across. Each seemed to have a starburst shape, deep in the center, with ridges and valleys around.

Neither man spoke for a minute as they swept their lights back and forth across the landscape. There was nothing else in sight, but they both realized what they were looking at.

"The tracks seem to head off this way," Jason indicated, pointing, "but it's hard to tell whether that's coming or going. There's no front or back to these things."

"If they went that way, that's toward the house. Do you think it, or they, were following the snowcat?"

"They've never shown any interest in people before, but..."

Without another word, both men spurred their horses and began to move as quickly as possible through the snow. As they rode, what had been a breeze began to grow into a wind, and blowing snow began to soften the deep tracks of the snowcat, now perhaps three miles ahead of them.

Chapter Eight

"HOW MUCH FURTHER do you think we have to go?" Sarah asked, squinting through the windshield of the snowcat. The glare of the headlights created a tunnel through a world of contrast. Bright white snow and the darkness of night made it hard to see much of anything.

"Maybe another mile or so, I think," Ashley replied. "We're getting close."

"I sure hope so. They've got to be freezing back there. The wind's picking up, too."

"I know. It's getting harder and harder to see my own tracks from the route out. They are almost buried already."

On the trailer, Anna was huddled low beside her son, holding his hand in the darkness. Only the barest reflection of light from the headlights gave any shape to the near white-out around her. Glancing around, she thought her eyes were playing tricks on her. It almost seemed that there were trees emerging in the darkness.

"How are you holding up, Michael?" she asked.

"I'm doing OK, Mom. It still hurts, but no worse than before."

Anna was glad that he was still conscious and gave his hand a squeeze. She had tried to monitor his pulse through his wrist, but it was too faint to find. Soon, though, he would be in a warm place, and medical professionals would be treating him, she told herself. He was going to be fine in the end. At least that's what she insisted would happen.

A moment later she glanced up and was convinced she had seen something moving behind them. 'That can't be Tom and Jason, they couldn't possibly keep up with the snowcat on horseback, we had too big a head start,' she thought. 'Who else would be out here?' She focused her attention, but really couldn't make out any more detail. Whoever was behind them, they were just far enough away that they tended to blend into the landscape. 'That's infuriating,' she thought. 'Are they just nosy neighbors? They could have helped.'

Just then she heard a shout from inside the cab of the snowcat. It was Sarah. "I can see the lights of an ambulance ahead!" she said, barely audible above the noise of the engine. Anna turned her head, and she could see the flickering lights, too. Help was only moments away.

Medical technicians rushed to assist as they drove into the yard of the ranch, and soon had Michael strapped to a stabilizing board. Eager to get him warm, they quickly him loaded into the ambulance and Anna climbed in beside him. In minutes they were headed toward the hospital, more than an hour away. Sarah and Ashley stood in the yard, watching them disappear.

"Well, I guess we should go inside and stay warm," Sarah said. "Tom and Jason should be along in a while. I think I'll put on a pot of coffee and whip up some hot food. I doubt they'll be sleeping any time soon."

"You go ahead, Sarah," Ashley replied. "I think I'm going to head home and park the snowcat. Mosely and Chuck drove down to Gallup this morning, and I want to check on the horses. They said they'd be back tonight, but with this snow, there's not much moving. I'll check on you tomorrow."

"Thanks, Ashley. I think you saved my brother's life tonight. I want you to know that I'm really grateful."

"You'd have done the same for me," she replied, and the two shared a warm hug.

"Now, off with you, you've got coffee to brew!" Ashley said, and climbed into the snowcat.

"Bye!" Sarah shouted as she started the machine. In a minute she had disappeared into the snow, which seemed to be turning into a genuine blizzard. Sarah hurried inside and began to prepare a meal for the men, happy that the night had ended so well.

•

Tom and Jason continued their hurried trot toward the house, still concerned about the tracks and the whereabouts of the creatures that had made them. Their horses did their best, but the snow made the going rough, and the growing wind had chilled them as well. "Come on, Spirit," Tom whispered to his horse, "Just a little farther, and there's a warm barn, and a reward for you tonight."

At last the barn loomed out of the darkness, and they dismounted in a pool of light from the floods. "I'll handle putting the horse up, Jason," Tom said. "Get yourself inside and warm up. You've had a rough night."

"Are you sure, Dad? I can help..."

"Just do as you're told, son. I'll handle this. I don't want you frostbitten."

Jason hurried inside, grateful to be out of the biting cold, but glad to see that the snow seemed to be slacking, at least for the moment. The wind had died slightly too. Maybe the worst of the weather was over. Inside the house, he quickly wrapped his hands around a steaming mug of Sarah's coffee and felt the bone-deep cold start to pass, only to be replaced by weariness.

Almost an hour had passed by the time Tom got the five horses unsaddled, fed, and set in their stalls. The details would have to wait for morning. He stepped out of the barn, happy to see that the snow had eased up. Still nervous about the tracks they had seen, he swept his eyes around the ranch, making sure that nothing was amiss. In the distance to the east he thought he could see an unusual glow. Stepping toward the fence, he realized that it was near the gate to the Circle M. 'Strange,' he thought to himself. 'I wonder what that could be.'

•

Ashley goosed the engine of the snowcat, eager to be back in the security of her own home. The events of the night had left her exhausted but running on adrenaline, and now it was fading. It was time to get some sleep. She drove the rig through the first of two washes, and felt it hesitate just a second as it climbed out. 'Oh, no,' she thought to herself. She hadn't had time to fill the tank before she dashed to the rescue, and now realized the gauge was pointing to 'E.' Just a little father, she thought, make it to home, and I can fill it tomorrow.

The cat purred on, but when it tried to climb through the second wash, the engine suddenly sputtered and died. "Dang it all," she said aloud to herself. "Now I've got to walk the rest of the way." She pulled her coat closer before opening the door and stepping out into the intense cold. Immediately she sensed something beside her, but before she could turn she was bodily lifted and spun. She screamed as she felt herself tossed like a doll and saw the ground racing by beneath. The solid strength of whatever had her was unrelenting. Resisting her efforts to escape, it merely squeezed her tighter. She felt herself being compressed, her breath forced from her lungs. She tried to turn her head to see what was happening, but felt blackness all around...

Chapter Nine

TOM STAMPED THE SNOW from his boots as he entered the mud room, and Sarah had a cup of coffee waiting when he stepped into the living room. Jason was already dozing in the recliner, blissfully warmer. "Thanks for the coffee, Sarah," he said, taking a sip. "It's perfect. How did you know I don't take sugar?"

"Just observant," she smiled.

Tom walked to pick up the phone. "I'm going to give Ashley a call, and make sure she made it home alright," he said, but quickly set it down. "Dead as a door nail. I guess the storm's taken the lines down somewhere between here and town. No surprise there. Have you seen my cell phone?"

"There's one on the table over there," Sarah said as she returned the cream to the refrigerator.

"Yeah, that's mine," he said, but then added after picking it up, "Of course, there's no signal, again. It's spotty enough out here in good weather, I shouldn't be surprised. Well, hell's bells, I just put the horses up, I sure don't feel like going back out there, but I noticed some lights in one of the washes. I'm worried that it could be the snowcat. I guess I'll have to go see."

"Do you want to wake Jason?" Sarah asked, grinning. "He wouldn't mind it, I'm sure."

"No, let him sleep, He's had a long day. I'll be back in twenty, twenty-five minutes."

Tom pulled his boots back on and slogged his way back to the barn through the snow, quickly saddling a fresh horse. His ride to the second wash took only ten minutes, but as he drew closer he was increasingly concerned. Even before he saw light shining from the open door of the snowcat, he had spotted the tracks in the fresh snow. A quick examination of the tracks around the cat made it clear that there were only three imprints that had been left by a human, and they led nowhere. The rest were the strange circles.

Quickly he dashed back toward the house, pulling his revolver and firing it twice as he rode. Jason was on the porch with his coat and hat by the time he got within earshot. "Saddle up! It's got Ashley!" he shouted," and Jason sprang into action, dashing to the barn. Tom turned and raced back in the direction of the snowcat. By the time he got there, he could already hear the hooves of Jason's fresh mount as he spurred it to a run.

Tom quickly assessed the situation as he rode. There was little chance of calling for help, and the snow had closed the roads to all but plows and snowmobiles. It would be up to Jason and himself. He scanned and followed the tracks as he counted what he had to work with if he went to battle with the beast. Because they'd seen the tracks earlier, he'd come prepared. His rifle was in its scabbard on the saddle, and he wore his old Colt on his hip. The revolver was a tradition he'd carried on from his father. He also had a police-style .38 in a saddlebag, and a few dozen bullets in a pouch, plus a large folding knife, and a small pocketknife. They would have to do, but they were untested against aliens. 'What if they have a force-field?' he thought wryly.

Within a half-mile Jason had caught up with him, and they quickly compared notes. Jason agreed that they needed to move fast, not wait for help. The images of the slaughtered cattle came to mind, and he tried to block them and focus on the challenge before them. "I brought my shotgun, Dad, but if it's got Ashley, we won't be able to use it."

"Let's just see if we can even keep up with this thing. It's got at least a half-hour lead on us, and we have no idea where it's going, or how fast it can get there."

Together the two set off at a near gallop, following a straight line of tracks that crossed the ranch. Jason half-expected them to head for the tunnel he'd found the year before, but instead they headed to a completely different part of the cliffs, farther west. He realized that they were almost backtracking to where they had been hours earlier.

At length the tracks came to a fence, and they were forced to stop and cut their own wire to get through. It appeared that their prey had simply stepped over it. "How tall is this thing that it can walk over a four-foot fence?" Tom asked.

"I'm not sure I want to know, really. We saw it crawl up that slickrock, but it was hard to judge size from that distance. If it stands like a man, I'd think it weighs more than two hundred pounds, judging by the depths of the tracks it leaves."

They had scaled the rocky slope at the foot of the cliff, and the horses were struggling to gain traction, when Jason stopped. "It looks like there's an opening in those rocks there," he said. "The tracks lead right toward it."

"Let's leave the horses," Tom said. "Bring your shotgun, and whatever else you can carry."

They climbed in the muffling snow on foot the rest of the way, carefully trying not to slip and tumble back down. Jason stopped and handed something to his father. "What's this?" Tom asked.

"It's a night-vision flashlight," Jason said. "Most animals can't see red light, and it won't mess up your night vision. I bought a couple of them a few weeks ago, but I hadn't used them yet. We'll see if they work on aliens."

The opening was little more than a tall crack in the rock. It was so narrow that Jason's shoulders brushed the stone of the walls as he entered in a crouch with his gun drawn. It appeared to be a natural cave, but soon widened to about ten feet, and sloped downhill. It had a flat floor that made walking easier, but was no warmer than the outside, thanks to a sharp breeze that followed them in. If the creature had any sense of smell, the two would never be able to sneak up on it, preceded by the smell of leather and gun oil.

Tom followed along the left wall as Jason kept to the right. They had gone about two hundred feet when suddenly they heard a sound, almost like a human voice.

"Ashley! Jason shouted. "Can you hear me?"

"Jason!" came the muffled reply, followed by a strange grinding noise. The two men dashed forward, only to be confronted by a wall of moving rock.

"Quick, it's closing!" Jason shouted, and dashed toward the disappearing slit of the door. With a thump it closed before him, and he slid into the stone face. "It's got her in there!" Jason screamed, and clawed at the edge of the stone with his fingers.

"Stop!" Tom shouted. "That's useless! That door is solid rock, and weighs tons. What I can see is ten feet wide and twenty feet tall. They make it move somehow, but we're not going to do it without dynamite, unless we can figure out the mechanism."

Quickly the two cast about, searching the walls, looking for any sort of control panel.

"There's nothing here but rock," Jason admitted at last. "They could use a remote control, or hell, thought waves for all we know."

"Then we're locked out," said Tom. "We lost."

"No! Don't say that! Ashley's alive, we're getting Ashley back, and I'm not stopping until we do!" Jason shouted.

"Great. What's your plan?"

Jason paused a moment. "There's another way in," he said, "and it doesn't know that we know about it."

Chapter Ten

ASON AND TOM RACED THEIR HORSES back down the mountain as fast as they could move through the deep snow. Still more had begun to fall, adding to the treacherous ride. When they were finally on level ground they split, Tom racing to Ashley's barn for three fresh horses, while Jason raced to their own ranch to retrieve his climbing equipment from their own barn. They met in minutes on the trail. Jason released his tired horse, mounted the fresh one, and together they headed for the strange tunnel Jason had found last year.

It took them almost an hour to negotiate the steep trail up the talus. They rode as far as possible, then left their horses to scramble the last few hundred yards through the blowing powder. Tom shone his light on the tunnel entrance, still thirty feet above their heads. "How are we getting up there?" he asked.

"I'll go first and toss you a rope," Jason replied. "Then I can pull up my duffle bag and drop it back down for you."

Tom watched as Jason used his arms and legs to brace himself against the curve of the rock face and scale the almost vertical slickrock. In less than two minutes he was there, and swiftly uncoiled the rope from his shoulder and fed it back to Tom. Soon both he and their gear were safely inside the tunnel. Jason opened his duffle bag and sorted through his gear, dividing it with his father. "We can move quickly from here, the tunnel's clear and flat," he said, flipping on his red flashlight. "I'll go first."

They made a virtual dash of the long tunnel, Jason silently counting his paces, and slowing before he approached the edge. At last it loomed before them.

"Now what?" Tom asked in a whisper.

Jason opened his pack and quickly strapped a climbing harness on himself, handing one to his father, who followed his lead. "Move to the opening, and help muffle the sound," he said.

Tom watched as Jason began to hammer pins into the sandstone, driving them through small metal clips. "I'm going to rig an abseil to lower myself," he told his dad, threading rope through the attached eyelets. "Watch very closely. These lines feed through here on your harness, then clip them with a carabiner like this. Use one of these cords to tie the line off like this and clip it to your leg straps. That's your safety brake."

Tom watched, repeating each step in practice. "Are you sure those little pins will hold your weight?" he asked.

"Normally I'd be driving a piton into a crack, but this is an artificial tunnel, and I don't see any sort of weathering cracks, but I found this tiny hairline. It will have to do. Once I get down there, I'll use my light to signal you. If I flash three times in a row, it means to come down. If I flash twice, it means I'm coming back up. I'll repeat each signal three times in a row. You can flash your light twice to let me know you read me."

Jason double-checked his rig and stuffed his pockets with extra gear. His hammer hung from his belt. With a slight pause, he braced his feet on the edge, put his back to the shaft, and began to lower himself down, walking on the nearly-smooth wall. In moments he was lost to sight. 'Please let this work,' Tom thought. 'He's my only son.'

Chapter Eleven

I T HAD BEEN A VERY LONG CHRISTMAS day, and was already after midnight when Sarah found herself alone the in the big ranch house after Tom's gunfire had led to Jason's sudden dash to the barn. 'I wonder what's up now?' she thought. She stood at the broad front windows of the house, staring into the snowy darkness. Fat flakes continued to fall, adding to the deep cover.

She had rarely found herself alone, and never before in a strange house on an isolated ranch far from home. It was a bit thrilling, but also a bit unnerving. Soon, she told herself, Tom and Jason would be back, and she could head to sleep. Until then, she would wait for a call from her mother.

She checked her phone for a text message, hoping to find an update on Michael's condition. They should soon be reaching a hospital, from what she had gleaned from the earlier comments from the EMT's, so word should be arriving soon. She picked up the land-line phone, but there was no dial tone. 'Somewhere there's a line down,' she thought. Moments later, the power went out, leaving her in almost total darkness. 'Great!' she thought. 'What else is going to happen tonight?'

She flipped on her phone flashlight and rummaged through the kitchen in search of candles and matches without success, before retreating to the living room where the dying embers of the evening's fire still cast a faint glow. She settled in to one of the comfortable reclining chairs with a blanket and was soon dozing.

Sarah couldn't tell how long she had been asleep when she woke with a start at the sound of something moving on the front porch. "Tom? Jason?" she called but got no response. She stared wide-eyed as someone, or something, tall walked slowly past the windows. The barely-perceived shape seemed huge and hunched. 'It must be a bear!' she told herself, huddling deeper into her blanket. Moments later she thought she heard a sound at the door, almost as if someone was trying to turn the knob…

Sarah sat frozen in fear, hoping against hope that Jason might have locked it on his way out. The strange looming shape that had passed before the windows was at least the size of a bear, so she was certain that it wasn't the men returning, or a neighbor coming to check on her at… She glanced at her cell phone, then realized that its glow might give her away. She huddled deeper into her recliner, pulling the blankets tighter. It was almost 3:00 am, and still there was no sign of Tom or Jason returning.

As she listened, she could hear the sound move from the side door to the kitchen windows. If only she could keep completely quiet, she thought, maybe it wouldn't know she was there, and go away. As she watched, the dark shape again mounted the porch, and as she stared she realized that it was not only tall, it was long, and crawling. She watched it pass close to her. 'At least ten feet!' she told herself. Did bears get that big? It was just at that critical moment that her cell phone suddenly rang. She quickly jabbed the button to silence it.

"Hello?" she whispered.

"Sarah, it's your mom, I'm really sorry to wake you but I couldn't reach Tom or Jason, neither of them…

"Mom, there's something here!" Sarah whispered urgently, cutting her off. "I'm alone, Tom and Jason had to go out…"

"Sarah, where are you?" Anna asked.

"I'm in the living room. It's outside on the porch, and its huge! It tried to get in the door, but I think it's locked."

"Listen to me, Sarah. Go into my room. There's a gun in the top drawer of the tall chest. It's got a lock, but there's a key on the nightstand. Do it now."

"Mom, there's no lights here, the power's out."

"Use your flashlight to find it, then try to call the sheriff. Stay in that bedroom, keep the door locked. I'm on my way."

Chapter Twelve

TOM WATCHED JASON DESCEND, passing slowly out of sight into the darkness of what seemed to be a bottomless pit. He noted when Jason's light came on, not flashing, but a steady examination of the wall below.

Jason looked around twice as he descended, at first making out nothing but unbroken stone walls. On his third inspection he thought he could make out a dark line below, He lowered himself another few feet and looked again. Yes, there appeared to be some sort of opening. It would be a risk, but he would have to drop in. Pushing with his feet, he swung away from the wall and lowered himself, swinging neatly into the alcove. Without disconnecting his ropes, he flipped on his light before stepping into the space. Almost immediately a glow lit the room, although he could discern no source. It was a large space, more than twenty feet high and at least seventy deep, and curved to match the round shaft. The walls, floor, and ceiling all seemed to be covered with the same slick surface. A row of doors led to individual anterooms around the outside of the curve.

Looking around, Jason noticed a tall doorway in the back of the room. His rope allowed him just enough slack to reach it. Beyond, a broad ramp sloped downward, also in a curve. He inspected the rest of the room to the reach of the light, noting only a strange array of horizontal shapes, like tall benches or low tables. 'Well,' he thought to himself, 'it's this or nothing.' He returned to the edge of the shaft, released his carabiners, and flashed his light to signal his father to descend. Within moments the ropes began to sway as Tom began his own, unsteady descent. When he appeared in the opening, Jason pulled the ends of the rope and left him seated neatly on the floor.

"That was fun, but I don't want to do it again," Tom said, looking just a bit pale.

"There's a way we can walk down from here," Jason told him, "but let's check the rest of this room first."

With weapons drawn they scouted around the chamber, which curved more than half-way around the shaft. At the far end they found a second ramp, this one ascending. "Looks like there may be another way out up there." Tom said. "Maybe we won't have to climb the rope."

"We can't let ourselves be caught in a dead-end, though," Jason replied. "Right now, the rope is the only thing I trust, and it's one at a time getting out of here" he added. "Unless we can confirm a route, I think we have little choice. Let's look down first. I'm pretty sure we're still higher than we were when we were in that cave."

Together the two walked cautiously down the sloping ramp, clinging close to the walls. As before, the space seemed to react to their presence, emitting a glow that lighted their way. Jason estimated they had descended about a hundred feet before they found a second room. The dimensions were similar to the first chamber. Every ceiling, every doorway, was at least twenty feet high or higher. There were dimly-lighted panels high on the walls, and faint lights twinkling from scattered locations around them. An array of colored discs added to the effect.

"This must be some sort of control room," Tom said, "but what do you think it controls? I really can't figure out the logic to any of this. Why is it all underground?"

"That's a good question. I only wish I knew the answers."

A quick scouting through the silence of this second chamber found no sign of life but revealed two new passages. One led still farther downward, and the second seemed to run horizontally, deeper into the mountain. "Which way should we go now?" Tom asked.

"We know that the entrance to this shaft is two or three miles from that cave entrance where we heard Ashley's shout. This passageway seems to lead back to the east if I still have my bearings. I vote for that."

"Then let's go," Tom said, and together they began moving down the hallway.

Except for the dimensions, it was almost like being back in the first tunnel. Unlike the circular proportions of the ventilation shaft, this passage was obviously meant for larger traffic. The twenty-foot ceiling and similar width gave it the feeling of space. Again, the walls and ceiling seemed to glow with a strange light that followed their passage, darkening again behind them.

"It's almost like St. Elmo's fire," Tom said. "Like a static electricity in the rock."

"Wait, something's coming!" Jason said suddenly."

"There's no place to hide unless we run back to that last chamber!" Tom said. "Should we just stand our ground?"

"We don't have much choice, but I don't think this is one of the predators we saw," Jason said, staring into the distance. "It's too small."

The two men waited, crouched against the wall, and watched the approach of a mechanical object, no more than three feet high. It rolled silently on wheels and didn't seem to recognize their presence. As it glided past they could see an array of tools mounted on folded or telescoping arms.

"That must be some sort of maintenance robot," Jason said.

"I'm glad it didn't take any interest in us," Tom said, "and I hope it's not reporting us back to headquarters. The lights coming on automatically is weird enough."

"It's all a bit unnerving, if you ask me," Jason said softly. "Like this place knows where we are. It could already be tracking our movements."

"At least if something else approaches, the lights should announce its approach. I'm keeping my eyes peeled on the tunnel ahead."

The pair walked in relative silence for another eight hundred paces, wondering where they could be heading. As before, the air was chilled to only a bit above freezing. "Damn, it's cold down here," Tom whispered. "I thought it'd be warmer inside all this rock."

"I have this theory that these things like it cold," Jason replied. "That's why they weren't around all summer."

Finally, after another two hundred cautious paces, they found themselves at the entrance to another dark and silent hall. They stepped slowly into the space, and light suddenly glowed from distant walls and ceilings. They realized that it was a large hall, perhaps five hundred feet across. The ceiling arced a hundred feet above, supported by a series of thick columns spaced across the room. Along the walls, rows of openings seemed to include both doors and window spaces, like a hundred eyes watching them. A second row of windows indicated another level above. Two of them were glowing.

"Quick, behind the column," Jason whispered, and they moved rapidly across the twenty feet to put the stone between them and the lighted windows. Lying flat on the floor, Jason crept to peer around the curve, trying to see if they had been noticed. Surely the sudden illumination of the entire hall wouldn't be missed by an observer. In a moment he saw movement, and quickly ducked back behind the column.

"There's someone up there, alright," he whispered, "I don't think we've been seen, though."

"Someone, or something?" Tom replied. "I'm ready to blast whatever we run into, and I don't like to think of these things as people."

"Well, they are apparently intelligent, even though they aren't human," Jason replied. "Somehow, though, I don't think we are going to be able to reason our way out of this. They have Ashley, and I want her back."

They waited briefly before rising to hurry into a room immediately below the lighted rooms they had seen. Quickly they scouted inside as it, too, began to glow, but found it empty.

"It's pretty had to be secretive when you're working under a moving spotlight," Tom said. "How can we possibly find Ashley without them knowing we're here?"

"I don't know, but I'm not quitting. I just hope a .45 can stand up to lasers or whatever sort of weapons they've got."

They peered cautiously through the window, hoping their movements hadn't been detected. A sudden sound made them both duck their heads. Outside, in the great hall, there was a patter of footfalls. Jason thought it sounded almost like a child running. If it was looking for them, the glow within their room would be a dead giveaway to their presence. Had they already been discovered?

Moving as slowly as he could, Jason leaned his head low and peered through the bottom of the doorway. He froze as he saw a sight that made his blood run cold.

The beast was only sixty feet away but wasn't moving. Its head was little more than terrible jaws raised above the bulk of its body on a short stalk of a neck. Yet it was the rest of the creature that shocked him the most.

When they had pursued it from a distance and seen the predator scaling the slickrock cliff far above, it was impossible to determine its size, and details were invisible. Now, up close, it was more frightening than his imagination had allowed. Perhaps twelve feet tall, its barrel-shaped body seemed to have branches. Jason saw with a shock that it had four 'arms' or upper limbs that reached to the ground. Around its center there were a double row of openings that he realized must be eyes.

It suddenly took several long strides in their direction, four sprawling legs giving the creature the appearance of a gigantic, thick-limbed spider. Jason suddenly understood how it had so easily scaled the cliffs, even carrying a load of beef.

"Here it comes, Dad. It's coming right at us, and it's ugly."

Chapter Thirteen

A NNA SPED THROUGH THE NIGHT, cursing the blowing snow that made driving treacherous. Everything, it seemed, was conspiring to slow her down. She had been forced to beg a ride from the hospital to the rental car company. She thanked her lucky stars for her 'platinum' status, and that she had thought to call before 11:00. She found the truck where they had said and unlocked it with the code they gave her. Sure enough, the keys were inside.

She cursed, too, the attitude of the deputy she had finally reached on her cell phone, after waiting what seemed to be an eternity for the emergency operator to connect her with the sheriff's office. Her first attempt had connected her to the wrong county office. "We can't handle that, it's outside our jurisdiction," she was told. "You need to ask for the Tamarisk County Sheriff's office."

The correct connection hadn't been much more use. "We already got a call on this, Ma'am. We don't normally run out there every time somebody sees a bear, Ma'am," the dispatcher had told her. "I'm sorry, but with the snow the way it is, I don't even know if I could get a deputy out there before morning."

The snow was certainly becoming Anna's biggest challenge. The road conditions had been bad before, closer to Farmington. Now they were just horrendous, and she was still on the paved highway. What she would find when she turned off might challenge even her rented four-wheel drive. The thought of some potentially alien beast stalking her daughter had her in shambles. Her imagination was making her crazy, and she found tears streaming down her face. 'Get a grip,' she told herself. 'You need to keep yourself clear-headed to deal with this.'

Anna tried to rationalize the fact that she hadn't been able to reach Sarah again and made up reasons she couldn't get through. 'The service on the ranch is spotty enough in good weather,' she told herself. 'It's no surprise that I can't reach her now. I was just lucky once. By now that bear is probably long gone, and she's sound asleep.'

The only good news she could be certain of was the positive report the doctors had on Michael. Tests had revealed no spinal injury, only two cracked ribs, and no sign of internal bleeding. The wound in his back had required a few stitches but should heal well. He was expected to be discharged tomorrow. Then she would have to make the long drive back. Hopefully, she thought, without any other complications.

Chapter Fourteen

TOGETHER THEY STOOD in the window facing the oncoming beast, the sill the height of their chests offering some protection. "Hold your fire," Jason said. "Don't shoot unless it attacks. If there's going to be a war, let them start it."

As the beast got within range, it suddenly swung what appeared to be a sort of scimitar. The sword clanged off the sill as the men ducked their heads, rising together to blast at the creature with their revolvers. Surprised, it seemed to stagger backwards, and then retreated.

"Well, that's encouraging," Tom said. "Now they know we're here, and we'll have to fight every step of the way. Unless, that thing's the only one, and we just drove it off or killed it."

"Not likely," Jason replied, "but let's move. We need to try to keep it, or them, off balance.

Together they dashed along the curving line of rooms, lighting each of them in sequence. At least if all were lit, they realized, it would be harder to track their location. Most of the rooms seemed to be small offices or perhaps bedrooms. None seemed to have rear entrances. As they ran they watched for any sign of the beast they had confronted. They had made it almost halfway around the room when a strange tone began to fill the air.

"Is that some sort of alarm?" Tom shouted over the growing din.

"It sure sounds like it might be. At any rate, we need to be ready. This place almost seems like a dead-end, I don't see another passage out of here!"

"There's something over there!" Tom shouted back. "I see an opening."

The two angled across the room, heading for the exit. They got there, only to realize that it was not one, but three converging corridors that entered the hall. They paused long enough to hear the patter of what sounded like a stampede of infants. They immediately recognized the source as the center of the three branching corridors and dashed to the left. "Wait a second," Jason shouted, and dashed back to enter the right corridor. It lighted in response before he ran back to join Tom. "Now let's go."

They ran, hoping that the beast, or apparently multiple beasts, that were now chasing them wouldn't be relying on sound or smell to trace them.

Jason estimated that they had sprinted for almost a quarter mile down the long corridor, and still he could hear the strange sound of pursuit. At length they found themselves in yet another of the large circular halls.

"It's like a gigantic ant colony," Tom said. "Which way now?"

"That way!" Jason said, and the room glowed as they continued their dash. Behind them they could hear a growing tumult that sounded almost like a river splashing. They both realized that it was the pattering of feet. They hadn't escaped yet.

"We need to find a place to make a stand, but more importantly, we need to find Ashley," Jason shouted as they ran, no longer trying to hide their passage.

"Where do we begin to look in this place?" Tom called back, lagging only a few feet behind. "It's huge, and we don't know where we're going!" Together they dashed into yet another forking corridor and ran only a couple of hundred feet before Jason called a halt.

"Let's see if we can discourage them," he said, and turned to face down the corridor. Tom quickly joined him, checking his revolver. "I just hope they don't have anything with a longer range than the sword that thing was waving."

"Did you notice, in that split second as we ducked, that the edge of it was glowing?" Jason said. "It looked metallic, but also had some sort of energy charge to it."

"I didn't get that clear a look," Tom said, "I was just trying to keep my head attached!"

Moments later the sound of pursuit grew louder, and several of the huge creatures burst into the tunnel in hot pursuit. Tom and Jason took aim and let fly a few rounds of lead. In the confines of the tunnel, even a missed shot could ricochet and do damage, and the creatures were confined without cover. They stopped for a moment in a near pile-up, then beat a hasty retreat.

"I think I counted six," Jason said as they turned to run, simultaneously flipping open his revolver to re-load.

"Let's hope that's all there are," Tom said, following suit. Both men had nearly emptied their guns, but neither could be sure they had done any damage.

Chapter Fifteen

THE EASTERN HORIZON was beginning to glow behind her when Anna finally turned her utility vehicle onto the long gravel road that led to the C9 Ranch. What had taken the ambulance ninety minutes to navigate the evening before had taken more than three hours to reverse. At least with growing light she was better able to stay on the road by following the fenceposts that stood half buried in the snow.

She passed the big house at the Circle M before she was suddenly brought to a halt by the sight of the snowcat. It stood almost blocking the road, snow drifted around it. At the sight of the open door she gasped. Someone had had an accident. Was the driver buried under that drift? Was it Ashley?

Anna leapt from her vehicle and ran the few feet to the snowcat. It was empty and seemed undamaged. Using her gloved hands, she began to probe rapidly through the snow drifted near the door and found nothing. The wind and blowing snow had erased any sign of tracks, and she realized she couldn't just search in the dark through every square foot of snow on the road, let alone the shoulders, or the adjacent pasture…

Quickly she gave up the search and drove on to the house, hopeful that Tom already knew about the accident or whatever it was, and that everyone was safe. If not, at least the group could search together.

The house seemed strangely dark when she arrived. There were still no lights. She parked the rental in the front yard and mounted the steps to the porch. Before she could reach the door, she noticed the strange patches of ice that seemed to form a pattern along the deck. She jerked to a halt and examined them. Those weren't bear tracks. They were more like uniform splatters, like…she looked around the yard, and saw parallel lines of circular impressions in the snow.

With a sudden panic she dashed to the door and began pounding on it. "Hello! she shouted. "Please, anyone, open the door! Can you hear me?"

Getting no answer, she ran along the length of the porch following the odd tracks and turned the corner to find the side door standing open. An odd green material was splashed across the deck, both inside and outside the door, where it appeared to be frozen. Looking, she could see that there was more of it mixed in the blowing snow. Suddenly cautious, she peered into the cold house. "Sarah?" she called loudly. "Sarah, are you here?" She thought she heard a sound from deep inside. She was unarmed, but if her daughter was in trouble, nothing would stop her. She stepped through the doorway.

Little seemed changed since she had left, except that the house, without power, seemed cold and empty. Was the beast that had made those tracks still hiding somewhere? She crept through the kitchen and all appeared normal, but in the living room a lamp was upset, and there was more mysterious green stuff, still in a liquid form. Glancing up the stairs, she saw nothing out of order. She crept slowly into the long hallway that led to the guest rooms, fearful of what she might find, trying to stifle her panic.

She checked doors as she passed, listening before opening them to peer inside. Nothing seemed amiss at all. At the end of the hall was her own room, the place of refuge she had recommended to her daughter. The door was ajar, and she realized with a start that there was a bullet hole in the door.

"Sarah?" she called, softly this time. Before she peeked through the crack. "Are you in here?" She thought she heard a muffled sound in response.

"Mom?" came a soft call. "Is that you?"

"Oh, my god, Sarah, are you alright?" she said, dashing into the room to find Sarah huddled in the closet, a gun in her lap.

"Sorry, I fell asleep. I think it's gone," Sarah said.

"What happened?" Anna asked, sweeping her into her arms.

"I had to shoot it. I'm sorry, I think it messed up the house. I wanted to clean it up, but I was too scared to leave the closet. I thought it might still be here."

Chapter Sixteen

T OM AND JASON CONTINUED TO RUN another hundred yards until they found themselves entering a series of smaller rooms facing the corridor. Nearly out of breath, they paused to listen for any sound of further pursuit. In the deathly silence that followed, Tom thought he heard a sound.

"Maybe my ears are still ringing from our shooting, but I thought I just heard something…odd," he said.

"I did too, but I couldn't tell where it came from."

As they stood gasping and listening, Jason suddenly froze. As Tom watched, a light suddenly seemed to shine on him. It was coming from a silently-approaching sphere.

"I hope we haven't pissed it off," Tom whispered. Jason didn't move.

After another few seconds, the light dimmed, and Jason spoke. "Let's go! Follow that thing."

The sphere quickly moved ahead of them, then zipped down the corridor faster than they could run. They followed behind, trying to keep it in view. At last it slowed to match their exhausted pace. It turned down a side corridor as they heard something approaching from ahead. After a series of corners, it seemed to arrive at its destination, and stopped before what appeared to be a sealed door.

"Ashley?" Jason called. "Are you there?"

"Jason!" came the muffled call from inside. "Please get me out of here!"

Already the two were feeling along the wall, trying to find any mechanism that might open the solid door. It fit neatly into the polished wall with only a hint of a separation. It seemed to be made of some sort of metal and had a strange greenish purple color. "It looks solid," Tom said, "and I don't see any sort of handle."

Jason turned to see the sphere still hovering silently nearby. "Please, if you understand me, show me how this thing works!"

Once again, the sphere glowed briefly. Jason stood upright and stared. "It says that I just have to want it to be open."

"Well, we already do, but it's not. There has to be more to this," Tom said.

Jason closed his eyes and concentrated, but nothing seemed to be working.

"Do it again," Tom said, and Jason gave it another try, this time with his hands on the door.

A moment later the door slid back, and Ashley rushed into his arms. He swept her to himself, swearing that he would never let go, but Tom quickly brought him back to reality.

"Come on, you two. We've got to find a way out of here, or we'll all be trapped in a cell like that. Or worse," he added.

The sphere led the way and they zig-zagged through a confusing array of new tunnels, each time listening for the telltale sound of splashing water that gave away the predators' footfalls. In ten minutes time they had seen no sign of the beasts but found themselves at the edge of yet another vertical shaft. Another curved room with another array of anterooms greeted them, but the only passage leading out led upward.

"Should we try this, or double back?" Tom asked.

"Before we do anything, maybe you should look up," Ashley said. They turned around to see her standing at the edge of the shaft. A glance surprised them both. At the top of the shaft far above them, daylight was visible. Jason realized with a start that they had been in the hellish maze for many hours, and it was a new day on the world above. Somewhere up there, the roof of the shaft had been broken or partially collapsed, perhaps in some ancient flood.

"How far up do you think that is?" Jason asked them. Tom and Ashley craned their necks to see the light streaming in, faintly glancing off the stone of the shaft.

"I'd say well over a thousand feet, maybe twice that, it's hard to say," Tom said. "That would be like climbing a skyscraper, maybe two. Is that our only option? What about the cave with the sliding door?"

"We have no idea where that is, and without the Messenger, no way of knowing," Jason replied. "Maybe that ramp is our best option."

Without another word Tom turned toward the ramp and began advancing, and as before the lights responded, illuminating the broad ramp. They climbed for minutes before coming to yet another of the mysterious curved rooms. A glance down told them they had gained more than two hundred feet. As before, there was another curved ramp sloping upward, and yet another horizontal passage. They resumed their climb but had only gone a short distance when Tom called a halt. "Listen," he said.

They paused long enough to hear the growing sound of a cascade above them. "That's not water," Jason said to Ashley. "Their feet have some sort of suction cups, I guess, and they make that squishing sound."

"OK," she replied. "Let's not worry about the details, let's just go the other way."

They hurried back to the room below and the horizontal tunnel. "This is a game of cat and mouse," Tom said as they began to move quickly down the corridor. "We're the mice, but the cats are the ones that know the territory. We need to change this game, or sooner or later they will spring a little surprise on us like they did your flying robot. They could be purposely herding us this way."

"Why is it so cold down here," Ashley asked. "Do they keep it this way on purpose?"

Behind, the sounds of pursuit had grown considerably louder.

"If my theory is correct," Jason said, "I don't believe they can function in warmer temperatures. That's why they have the ventilation shafts, so they can pull in cold winter air, and vent heat in the summer."

"They're catching up to us!" Ashley shouted.

Tom glanced backward. The long, straight tunnel glowed with its unearthly light, he could see a distant jumble of movement, dozens of legs striding rapidly toward them. "We need to find a place to make a stand," he said.

"Let me see if I can discourage them again," Jason said. "Keep going, I'll catch up." He paused and knelt, steadying his arm to aim into the center of the pack of creatures. He fired off two rounds and saw a momentary confusion as at least one of the beasts stumbled. The rest kept coming. "There's too many of them," he shouted as he raced behind. "I don't have enough bullets left to stop that pack."

Ashley and Tom were now nearly two hundred feet ahead, and as Jason ran he saw them make a sudden turn. Tom paused to be sure they had been seen, waving his arm to signal. "Keep going!" Jason shouted.

As he reached the turn, Jason realized that it was another of the shafts. Was it the same one they had been in earlier, or a different one? Hadn't they changed levels? The maze was so confusing he wondered how the beasts had learned to navigate it. He dashed across the curved space that hugged the precipice and followed Tom's voice to the left into another of the spiraling ramps. Behind he could hear the pack gaining on him rapidly. His lungs ached, and his ribs were cramping. Soon, he knew, they would have to stand and fight.

Chapter Seventeen

ANNA SAT ON THE CLOSET FLOOR for a few minutes, cuddling and consoling her daughter. The guilt she felt at bringing her children to this place, and exposing them both to danger, gave her serious qualms about her suitability as a mother and single parent. Now her son was hospitalized, and her daughter had been forced to defend herself against an unknown and likely alien attacker, alone in the dark. She resolved to do better

"Mom, how's Michael?" Sarah asked. "I kept trying to call you to find out last night, I've been so worried."

"He's going to be fine," Anna told her. "They expect to discharge him later today. He'll be hurting for a few days, but he'll be as good as new soon." Just then, the lights came on.

"Oh, they fixed the power!" Sarah said. "I hated the dark last night."

"What did you see, Sarah?" Anna asked her. "What came into the house? Was it a bear?"

"I couldn't really see much in the dark," she replied. "I thought it was a bear. I yelled at it, but it didn't run. When it tried to come into the room, I shot at it twice."

"Well, you may have hit it. You did the right thing," Anna said.

"Thanks, I was afraid you'd be mad because I shot a gun in the house."

Anna smiled and shook her head. "Honey, do you think you can get up?" she asked. "Come on, I can make breakfast for us."

"But Mom, what about Tom and Jason?" Sarah asked as she rose. "Where are they? Do you think they're OK?"

A sudden sound from the front of the house stopped Anna's response. Both women turned to look through the open bedroom door, and Sarah reflexively grasped the gun. Slowly, and as quietly as possible, Anna rose, took the gun from Sarah's hands, and crept toward the hall. At the sudden sound of running water she froze. Jason had described exactly such a sound.

Cautiously Anna moved into the long hallway, and closed the door behind her, leaving Sarah inside. She would face any threat alone. The sound of a door, opening and closing, was followed by soft humming. Anna crept down the hall and peeked into the living room. Juanita was busily mopping up the strange green stains.

"Oh, thank goodness it's you!" she exclaimed.

"Good morning, Anna," Juanita cheerfully replied. "I'll be cooking up some breakfast soon, but there's coffee brewing now, I just need to clean up this mess first. It looks like somebody spilled something here." Then she noticed that Anna had a gun in her hand, and her expression changed from smiling to worried. "Is everything OK?" she asked.

"It is now," Anna told her, "but we're not sure where Tom and Jason are off to. They left in the middle of the night, and I saw Ashley's snowcat in the road."

"I saw it too, on the way here," Juanita replied, returning to her mopping. "I checked, it looks like it's out of gas."

Anna nodded at the explanation. "Let me get myself together and get Sarah," she said. "I'm looking forward to your coffee." She returned to the bedroom and found Sarah waiting at the door. "It's all clear," Anna told her, "but no sign of the men."

The two women were soon in the dining room sipping steaming mugs of coffee as they related to Juanita the traumatic events of the evening before, and her long drive to the hospital and back. "Also, there was some sort of intruder last night, an animal that came into the house," Anna explained. "That's what left the mess on the floor. I'm going to try calling Ashley now. I'm very worried, because if there was a wild animal here, it could have gone after her earlier." she added.

Anna soon discovered that the land-line was still out, even though the power had been restored. "I can't get a signal to call Ashley's cell phone, either," she said after a few attempts. "I think I need to go over there and see if she's OK."

"But Mom, you've been up all night, driving. At least I got some sleep," Sarah said. "Let me go check. You need your rest."

At the mention of sleep, Anna suddenly felt the weariness she had been suppressing. "No, I won't let you go alone, but I'll let you come along. You can drive, if you don't mind. I've got an SUV outside with all-wheel drive."

"OK, but then you need to sleep," Sarah told her.

They had barely set out for the Circle M when Sarah realized that her mother had already dozed off in the front seat. She smiled, then slowed to pass the abandoned snowcat. A few fat flakes of snow were falling in the diminishing wind, but there were footprints visible around the vehicle. When she finally got to the entrance drive to the Circle M, she realized that the snow was undisturbed. The big vehicle struggled but managed to make it through the foot of fresh powder.

Carefully removing the gun from her sleeping mother's hand, Sarah stepped from the car and approached the house. Ringing the bell brought no response, nor did her loud knocks on the solid wood of the front door. Peering into the interior through the front window, she saw no sign of life.

Sarah walked into the center of the yard, lifted the gun, and fired a shot into the ground. Within seconds she heard a commotion from the bunkhouse about a hundred yards away.

"Hey!" came a shout from Mosely as he emerged, clad in a dark parka. "Everything OK?"

"We can't find Ashley, or Tom or Jason, either!" Sarah called. "I'll be right there!"

"We thought she was still in the house," Chuck told her when she had caught up with them racing toward the barn. "I figured she wouldn't be out and about so early with all this snow."

"She never made it home last night," Sarah replied. "We found her snowcat in the dip on the road. It's out of gas. Tom and Jason left to find her last night, and they never came back, either."

"We got back from Gallup last night as the storm was getting heavy," Chuck told her. "I figured we might get snowed in. We hit the hay, never heard a thing. I guess the power was out, too? Clocks are off."

"Yes, and the phone is still out," Sarah told him. "I'm not sure about the cell, I can't seem to get through right now."

"It almost never works," Mosely said. "Well, we need to get searching for them, now. As soon as someone can raise help, we'll get a posse together, but for right now it's just us."

Chuck and Mosely knew, probably better than Sarah, that hypothermia killed people almost every time they got a heavy snow, leaving cars stranded on rural roads, or buried in drifts. Most victims were from the city, inexperienced with the back country and unprepared for the weather, not experienced ranchers. What, they wondered, could have led the three of them to disappear on such a night?

Inside the horse barn they got another surprise. "That's Tom's horse!" Mosely said, pointing at a stallion in the first stall.

"Where's Curley?" Chuck asked. "Two-bit and Munchkin are gone, too."

"It looks like Tom came back during the storm for some fresh horses," Mosely said. "That's our first clue to where they went."

"I'll go back and raise the hands from the C9," Sarah said, "but I don't know where we can even start."

"I'm pretty sure I know," Mosely said grimly. "If they needed fresh horses, they were heading up-country," he added.

It took less than ten minutes for Chuck and Mosely to saddle up and load their gear. They included their rifles, packed in their scabbards, and each wore a side arm as well.

"We're heading up along the cliffs," they told Sarah as they mounted up. "If you can get through to the sheriff, let him know we've got some missing folks up here. He'll round up some more help and follow our trail."

"Thanks, and good luck. I'll keep trying to get through," she called to them as they rode off, as fast as the deep snow would allow.

Chapter Eighteen

SARAH CLIMBED BACK INTO HER VEHICLE and fired it up, heading back down the drive toward the road and the C9 bunkhouse. The bunkhouse was half a mile south of the main house, nestled between two large barns. The snowy landscape glistened in the morning light as the thinning clouds finally let the sun begin to filter through, making it an idyllic scene. The last flakes of snow were still sifting gently down, but Sarah was glad to note that the wind had nearly died. Anna was still asleep when she pulled up next to the bunkhouse. She knew the ranch normally had two men, but she'd never met them. She hoped they were home. Anna was still sleeping when she ran to knock on the door.

"Well, come on in, little lady," a man said as he opened the door.

"I can't, I've come for help, to tell you that Tom and Jason are missing!"

"What do you mean, they're missing? Who are you, and how would you know?" he asked, looking at her skeptically.

"I'm staying with them, in the house, with my family…" she stammered.

"Well, why don't you come in, and tell me all about it," the man suggested. "It's too cold for me to stand here in the doorway."

"No, I really can't, I need to go help search for them," Sarah replied. "If you won't come help, then I'll go alone," she said, and began to turn away. In an instant the man snatched her wrist and jerked her sharply backwards into the doorway.

"I don't believe that we finished our little chat yet," he said, grinning at her.

Sarah turned and punched the man as hard as she could in the throat. He staggered, but rather than releasing his grip on her wrist, he grasped her other wrist and pulled them together. His grip was strong, and he pinned her wrists together with a single hand. Sarah dropped to the ground in the doorway, screaming at him to let go, but he began to pull her into the bunkhouse. She kicked and screamed, but he managed to get her through the door, and turned away to kick it closed behind them. It didn't move, and the man glanced back to find himself staring into the barrel of Tom's .38 caliber pistol, clenched firmly in the grip of a very angry woman.

"I'm going to give you to the count of three to let go of my daughter. Get on your knees, now!" Anna shouted at the man.

Wide-eyed, he released Sarah and dropped to his knees. "Please don't shoot, I wasn't going to hurt her," he begged.

Sarah gathered herself and stood next to the cringing man. With a swift kick she connected with his groin. He screamed, and Anna fired a shot into the wooden floor next to him that had him rolling backwards in both terror and agony.

"Once we find our friends, I'm coming back to deal with you," Anna told him. "Are you alright, baby?" she asked Sarah.

"Yeah, Mom," she said. "Just shaken, and my hand hurts from punching him, but I'll be fine. Let's get out of here."

Sarah walked out the door, and Anna turned back to the cowboy on the floor. "Remember my promise. I'll be back," she said, and followed Sarah to the car.

They drove away in silence, their hearts pounding. "Thank you, Mom. I love you so much!" Sarah said at last.

"Honey, in my world, we stand for family," Anna replied.

They reached the main house in minutes, and quickly checked the phone. The line was still dead, and their cell phones still had no signal.

"Should I try to drive toward town to see if I can get a connection from there?" Sarah asked Juanita.

"It's worse toward our place, and that's four miles closer to town," Juanita told her. "I barely made it through to get here this morning. Beyond our house, you would have to climb the ridge, and then it's another eighteen miles to Lickton. I don't think that road will be open for a while, they don't normally get around to plowing it until two or three days after a storm like this. The county only has one plow, and it's a low priority. We just have to wait until there's a signal."

"Since Mosely and Chuck are already out there, I don't know what we should do right now," Anna said.

"I think you should stay right here for a while and get some rest," Juanita told her. "I've got some experience with how things work on the ranch. Eat first, then take a nap. I already cooked up some breakfast, and you are going to need your energy if they don't come back soon."

"I don't think there's anything we can do right now but rest up, in case we're needed later," Sarah agreed. "Let's do what she suggests. Get something to eat and hit the hay."

"I guess you're right," Anna admitted. The burst of adrenaline that had brought her to alertness was already fading, and her weariness had returned. "I will, but only if you'll let me know any news. If you leave me sleeping again I'll never forgive you," Anna said.

"I promise," Sarah told her.

"I'll wake both of you," Juanita added.

Thirty minutes later, both had eaten some of the feast Juanita had prepared and were already sound asleep.

The morning passed slowly. Juanita walked outside every few minutes to try to get a cell signal. Normally poor, today there was none. 'Only time will tell,' she thought to herself.

Chapter Nineteen

C HUCK AND MOSELY MOVED SLOWLY along the irregular base of the cliffs, heading steadily west. They passed the fence into the C9, periodically scanning the high country with their field glasses. At last they came upon the nearly buried tracks that must have been made by horses passing, all but buried in last night's blowing snow. They hurried their horses, and gradually the trail became fresher, a bit clearer. It was heading westward, and toward the cliffs.

Twenty minutes later they came upon three horses, still saddled, and standing together in the snow, loosely tethered to a bush. They could see before they arrived that they were their own missing Curley, Two-bit, and Munchkin.

"Looks like they headed off on foot going that way," Chuck said. "You can see where their tracks lead up that slope."

"Then we've got to head that way ourselves," Mosely replied. "I'm going to try again to call for some help."

As Chuck grabbed some gear, Mosely made repeated efforts to gain a signal, holding his phone aloft, and pointing it in different directions.

"Nothing," he said at last. "I thought that from up here, at least, we might be able to get a signal on this thing"

"We've got to go on, help or no help," Chuck said. "If the girl gets through, they'll be able to pick up our trail easily enough. They'll find us."

The two cowboys set out on foot up the steep slope, made even more treacherous by its blanket of snow, which concealed the stones and irregularities. For half an hour they scrambled upwards following the trail left by Tom and Jason, until at last they came upon the ropes that dangled from the opening in the rock.

"There's no more tracks past this point, so it looks like they went in there." Chuck said with surprise, "but why on earth they did, in the middle of this storm, has got me completely stumped!"

"It would be one way to get out of the cold and snow," Mosely told him, "but I can't imagine why they would come all this way to do that. At least if they're in there, they're probably safe and reasonably warm. Let's get them out."

•

With the pack of predators quickly gaining on him, Jason turned to see the Messenger leading the way down the corridor. It seemed to know every inch of the vast space, and they were completely reliant upon its guidance. They dashed after it, hoping that it would lead them to a quick exit. In minutes they passed through two more cavernous halls, and traveled up a long, spiraling ramp. As they passed down a long hall with intersecting passages, Tom and Jason were so disoriented that they had no idea whether they were passing places they had been, or completely different sections of this honey-combed mountain.

After running for several minutes longer, all of them were becoming a bit winded. The Messenger had gotten farther ahead and paused a moment to wait for them. Suddenly one of the enormous predators stepped into the corridor between them. Ashley shrieked in horror at her first real glimpse of one of her kidnappers, but the beast had it's back to them, and did not turn. Instead, it strode toward the Messenger. From beyond, the trio could see another of the creatures advancing toward it as well, trapping it between them. Then with a single stroke of a scimitar blade, the sphere was sliced neatly in two, the concealed mechanical parts of the robot vehicle smashing against the wall and floor. Slowly the beast turned around to face them, and emitted an ear-shattering, high-pitched scream. Already Tom and Jason had their revolvers drawn to face it down when Ashley screamed again as the pursuing pack began to stream down the corridor behind them.

Jason looked at his father, grabbed Ashley's hand, and began to charge at the single beast in front of them. It seemed surprised, and more so when both men fired off rounds at close range. The creature staggered and howled in pain or surprise before falling back into the passage from which it had emerged. In another moment they sprinted past it, noting the trail of green liquid on the floor. There was still one more of the beasts blocking their forward passage, but two more shots left it also fleeing the charge. All three of them dashed past it, and Jason paused to make certain there was no close pursuit.

Behind them the pack seemed to have become less motivated, perhaps leaderless, but Jason realized that they really had no idea where it was they were going, and without their guide, they remained the quarry of an unknown number of predators.

In less than two minutes they reached what appeared to be another control room, as before lined with the dimly-lit panels and colored discs. As Jason caught up with Tom and Ashley, he found them both virtually collapsed, panting from their long run. "Dad," he gasped. "We've got to fight. None of us can run much farther."

"This is the place, then, Jason." Tom said. "Let's do this."

Jason collapsed on the floor, again drawing his gun to reload. He glanced at his diminished supply of ammunition. "I've got about fifteen more rounds, and I'll be done," he said aloud.

"I've got a couple dozen," Tom answered, checking his own pouch. "How many do you think there are?"

Ashley's face was a pale mask as she stared at the opening behind them. "They're coming," she said, "and there's lots of them."

Chapter Twenty

"MOM, I'M SORRY TO WAKE YOU, but something's happened," Sarah said softly.

"What? What is it?" Anna said, suddenly sitting up in bed. "What time is it?"

"It's almost noon," Sarah answered.

"So, what's going on?" Anna demanded, climbing out of bed and pulling on her jeans.

"Jason's horse is here. I recognized the saddle. It just came walking along alone, heading for the barn."

"Oh, god no, that's not good!" Anna said, scrambling to dress and pull on her boots.

In a moment Anna had finished dressing and dashed down the hall. "Juanita, can you pack us some cold food?" she said. "We need to take a ride, and we may not be back for a while."

"Yes, Ma'am, I already fixed something up, a trail lunch, enough for eight people. It's in this bag," Juanita answered. "You'd best be dressing warm, though, it's mighty cold out there, and getting colder later."

113

Anna nodded, going down a mental checklist. "Sarah, can you fill some canteens? There's a few spares in the mud room, and we're going to need water…oh, and grab a first aid kit, some lights, matches, anything else you can think of. Then get into your warmest clothes. We may be out in the cold for a long while. I'm going to go saddle up some horses."

Anna dashed to the barn and found Jason's horse standing outside. She opened the door and brought it in, removed its saddle, and quickly checked it over. 'No injuries,' she thought to herself. 'That's a good sign.' It was all the reassurance she could find, but she clung to it.

She chose two of the remaining horses and saddled them, adding saddle bags to hold the gear they might need. She took another coil of the lightweight nylon climbing rope that Jason stored in the barn and added that to the pack. Once she was ready, she brought the horses to the house. "Load what you have while I change into something warmer," she told Sarah. "Then we're going to go do what we can to help."

•

Chuck and Mosely stood at the foot of the cliff face for two minutes hollering their loudest calls, trying to attract a response from the cave. Giving up on the shouting, Mosely drew his pistol and fired three shots in quick succession, prompting a dusting of snow to cascade from the cliffs above. Still they got no response.

"Do you think we can get up there?" Mosely asked.

"I'm pretty good at throwing a rope, and I can lasso 'most anything," Chuck answered, "but I never tried climbing one since I was a kid. But if you want to give it a go, I'm game."

"I just wish't I'd worn better boots for climbing. I'm not used to this stuff," Mosely observed. "That slickrock don't look like it's gonna' offer much traction for these things," he said, nodding toward his pointy-toed cowboy gear.

It took the two nearly half an hour to get up to the hole, after several failed attempts. Chuck dragged himself up the rope, and then managed to pull Mosely up after him as he clawed at the rock from his half-dangling position.

"Dang, I wouldn't want to try that again anytime soon!" Mosely said, panting at the entrance to the tunnel. "That near scared me half to death. I don't know if I ever told you I'm afraid of heights."

"Yeah, that, and cow-eatin' monsters," Chuck grinned at him.

"That was no imagination," Mosely reminded him. "You'd better be keeping your gun handy if that thing's living in this hole."

Chuck fumbled for his phone and turned on the flashlight. Cautiously the two men advanced a short distance into the passageway before Mosely stopped. "I got a bad feeling about this, Chuck. This ain't no cave. Something's gone and dug this, bored it right into the rock. It's smooth, and it runs straight as an arrow."

"I'm with you on that, Mose," Chuck replied. "But to me, that just proves that it weren't an animal that made it. Somebody came up here before and made this, like a mine shaft."

"If you say so, but I never heard of a mine in this slickrock, and it's got no supports, no rails, nothing that says 'mine' to me."

The two men walked another short distance before Chuck called a halt. "My phone's getting low on juice already. I didn't expect to be walking in a cave like this. You got any charge in yours?"

"Yeah, I never use the danged thing," Mosely replied. "I'm not even sure why I carry it, can't even call the house, 'cause there's never any signal."

"Well, it's gonna come in handy if we need to find our way back out of here," Chuck said.

"It's just a tube, so far," Mosely offered. "We could do that in the dark if we had to."

"Maybe you could, but I'm…I don't like walking in the dark," Chuck said.

"Wait, are you afraid of the dark, Chuck, ol' buddy?" Mosely asked, grinning. "That's why you keep that night light in the bunkhouse?"

"It's no worse than you and your bogeyman," Chuck replied. "'I think I gotta be moving on' and all that."

"I'm telling you, what I saw weren't no bogeyman, it was a big-ass animal, and you'd'a been scared, too," Mosely assured him.

"Well, just keep your light handy, we're getting pretty far down this hole, and there's no end in sight."

"Um, Chuck, I just checked my phone," Mosely offered. "I got forty percent."

"Forty percent? That's all?" the cowboy asked.

"Yep. Guess'n' I never plugged it in last night."

"So what do you reckon we should do? Keep going, or turn back?" Chuck asked.

"Want to try hollering again?"

"Sure, why not."

The two men raised their voices and called out, but the tunnel seemed to swallow the sound, not a hint of an echo returning to their ears.

"Maybe it just goes on forever," Chuck offered.

"It may, but I'm not," Mosely replied. "I'm only going far enough to find Tom, and Jason, and Miss Ashley."

"Then that's where I'm going too," Chuck answered.

Chapter Twenty-one

"I'LL HOLD THEM OFF if you want to try to make another break for it," Jason said.

"No," Tom said. "We stay together."

It took only moments for the pack of predators to reach the entrance to the control room. Tom and Ashley stumbled to the far end of the room, and Jason aimed his revolver, expecting the pack to rush them immediately. Instead, they drew to a halt. Jason could see their grotesque legs at the entrance of the corridor. He waited, but nothing seemed to be happening. The beasts seemed suddenly cowed, and Jason thought he heard footsteps retreating. "Why aren't they still coming after us?" he said. "Are they afraid of something in this room?"

"What's that other sound?" Ashley asked, and everyone fell silent. A distant whooshing noise was growing quickly louder.

"Don't tell me there's something worse coming?" Tom said. "It sounds almost…mechanical."

The noise grew in intensity, and the three of them huddled in a corner of the room next to the window. Jason kept an eye on the tunnel where the pack had been, while Tom and Ashley stared at the second, which seemed to be the source of the sound. The noise grew to a dull roar, and a machine suddenly squeezed its bulk through the corridor and entered the room. A squarish block, it bristled with telescoping arms that quickly extended brushes to the walls and ceilings all around, while a broad flange in front seemed to conform to the width of the floor.

"It's some sort of cleaning machine!" Tom shouted above the roar. "Get your heads down!"

There was no time to escape, so the three huddled behind the low wall as a sudden burst of wind hit them. The machine seemed to sense their presence, and swept over and around them, quickly continuing around the room. They watched it depart, fascinated.

"That's why those predators ran. They're afraid of that thing!" Jason said.

"Like my cat and the vacuum cleaner," Ashley said.

"Then I've got an idea," Tom said. "Follow me!" He rose and ran after the machine, which was already disappearing down the opposite tunnel. Ignoring the loud roar, he managed to catch up to it, and climbed onto the back of the machine, pulling Ashley's hand to help her alongside. Jason jogged behind, surprised at the audacity of the move. If it would keep them safe, it made sense. The machine hesitated only a moment, as if recalculating the new weight. A moment later, Jason climbed aboard as well, the three of them huddled on the small space above the machinery.

"If we're safe here, can we just stay?" Ashley said above the noise.

"I don't see why not," Tom answered her. "We didn't know where we were going before, and we still don't."

"Thank you for coming to find me," she said. "I can't believe that you did."

"We could no more leave you down here alone than jump over the moon," Jason said, smiling at her. "You have a lot to live for." Tom smiled and nodded.

Ashley closed her eyes, and in moments seemed to fall asleep, her head resting on Jason's shoulder. The sight reminded the men that they hadn't slept in many hours and were running on adrenaline alone. With a chance to relax, all three were asleep in minutes as they were borne to an unknown destination.

Chapter Twenty-two

"HELLOOOO!" The sound echoed faintly from far below but brought no response.

Chuck and Mosely stood at the edge of the abyss, looking down the length of the ropes that still dangled there. "I can't see how far the ropes go, but that must be where they are, down there, somewhere," Chuck said. "As far as lights go," he said, waving his phone, "this thing is about as useless as they come."

Mosely pondered their situation a moment. "I'm no good at climbing ropes, and if I tried to slide down that thing I'd probably just slip off and fall. That would do them no good, and me less," he said wryly. "I think we need to try a different approach. Let's try to figure out what's going on."

"I'm with you, Mose," Chuck replied. "I can't imagine anyone willingly going down there, so I'm stumped as to why they did."

"Sarah said that all three of them were gone, but that Ashley's snowcat ran out of gas," Mosely said. "I'm guessing that something got her, and that Tom and Jason went down there trying to get her back."

"You think something snatched her and took her down this hole? What on earth…" Chuck paused. "You think it was that thing you saw, don't you? Your abominable snowman, or whatever it was."

"It weren't no abominable snowman, Chuck, don't make light of this," Mosely replied. "I know what I saw, and it weren't no animal either of us ever laid eyes on before. If it could make off with a thousand pounds of beef, it could sure run off with Ashley, she can't weigh more'n one-twenty, soakin' wet."

"Well, that's true," Chuck admitted. "So, if your theory is right, Tom and Jason are down that hole, and they are going to have to fight the thing you saw to get her back." He almost added, 'if she's still alive,' but thought better of it.

"Yes, that's what I think, and what's more, I think they've been down there for a good while now. Maybe since midnight, or not long after." He glanced at his watch. "That's around twelve hours. We need to do something serious, and we need to do it fast."

"But what, Mose?" Chuck asked. "What can we possibly do from here?"

•

Jason slept a dreamless sleep but awoke with a start to…silence. His sudden movement instantly disturbed his huddled sleeping companions. Clearing the fog from their minds, they looked about. They were still atop the machine, apparently parked in some sort of small garage, just barely large enough to house it.

"Thank goodness for this robot thing," Jason said. "Otherwise we'd probably never have survived last night."

"Was it last night?" Ashley asked. "How long have we been sleeping? How long have we been down here? I have no sense of time."

"I wish I knew. I haven't worn a watch in a few years, I always relied on my phone," Tom said.

Jason fumbled in his pocket. "My phone's almost out of juice, but it says it's 10:18. I guess it's already tomorrow?"

"I'm hungry and thirsty," Ashley said. "I hope we can get out of here soon."

Jason removed the small pack that still held his climbing gear and pulled out three energy bars. "It's all I keep in here, but it'll have to do, unless you want to try grilling one of those predators."

"Uh, no thanks," Ashley replied. "I think I'll make this last a while."

"I've only got a sip left in my canteen," Jason added.

"I've got a few swallows in mine, but that won't last us long," Tom said. "I'm too parched to eat. We've got to get out of this maze or find water. But I think our immediate problem is, how do we get out of this room?"

At that statement, all three began to scan the walls. Only the barest crack revealed a door at all, but no sign of any sort of handle.

"What's that colored disc on the wall up there?" Ashley asked, pointing.

"Don't know," Tom said. "We saw lots of those in the control rooms, but they're pretty far up the wall."

"Can you boost me up there," Ashley asked.

"Here, I can," Jason replied. "You'll have to stand on my shoulders to reach it." He squatted next to the wall as Ashley carefully balanced, and then straightened up to a standing position, raising Ashley ten feet from the floor. Stretching, Ashley reached and touched the disc.

Immediately the wall opened, the entire mass of stone gliding smoothly out of place.

"Just like in that first cave we went in yesterday…or the day before," Tom said. That's how they control these things. I guess it makes sense to have controls up high if you're twelve feet tall."

"Remember," Jason said. "These creatures didn't build this place, according to the Messenger, so whatever did must have been tall, too."

"Good point," Tom said. "Anyway, we're free, let's get out of here."

The three scampered out of the room, leaving the door standing open. They were in what appeared to be a large service alcove, which opened onto a large hall. They stepped cautiously forward. Above their heads tiers of structure soared for a hundred feet, and seemed to support some sort of hanging garden of greyish plant-life.

"What it that stuff?" Tom asked.

"I think this is a farm," Jason said. "If I had to guess, I'd say it might be a sort of fungus. It can't be any sort of normal plant because there's no sunlight down here. And it's really cold, so it's probably adapted to life on some other planet. Should we try to get a sample?"

"Let's not worry about that right now," Ashley said. "You can get extra credit in Anna's class after we find a way out of here."

Jason nodded and scanned the rest of the room. More glowing panels lined the end wall near them, but none had any discernable displays.

"Let's try to use our heads, now that we're not being attacked, and have had some sleep," Jason said. "What's the purpose of all these panels, if they don't show anything? And why are they below the control buttons up there? Can we learn anything from them?"

Tom stepped forward and touched one of the panels, and it began to respond, a series of strange marks appearing on the screen. He touched it again, and a strange diagram appeared. It immediately assumed depth, and a complex hologram appeared to penetrate the wall behind. "What do you make of that?" he asked.

"Is it some sort of map?" Jason said. "It could be a three-dimensional representation of this space."

"Like the 'you are here' maps in the mall in Denver?" Ashley asked.

"Let me try something," Jason said, and swept his hand across it. Immediately the image changed, and a glowing dot appeared.

"It's simpler now, maybe only 2-D," Jason said. "If that's the case, we are in the center of the complex. Or…it just shows what is around us."

"If this is 2-D," Ashley said, "and this is just this level, are those the corridors, and those things the rooms? And what are these nodes with the colored marks?"

Jason peered closely at the screen, trying to make sense of the confusing array of lines and shapes. "I'm not certain, but if we're here, and that space is the garage where we left that cleaning machine," he said, pointing at the screen, "we must be facing this direction. I wonder if they put north at the top on their maps."

Tom chuckled a bit at that. "Well, son, I doubt they expected us to be standing here trying to figure it out, so it's probably not that simple. But let's head to this node," he said, pointing, "and see if we can find out what it represents."

With no sign of any predators, the trio walked as quietly as possible down the long corridor. Jason and Tom kept in mind the sudden appearance of the beast that had destroyed the Messenger, but the polished walls gave no hint of any side openings. At length they reached the expected node. There they found more lighted screens and colored discs high on the walls. Ashley immediately stepped to a screen and touched it, and again an image appeared.

"It looks like we were right, it shows us in the new location. Let's try to get to the 2-D screen again," she said.

Jason admired her as she stretched to manipulate the screen. 'I'm never leaving this woman,' he told himself.

Soon she had found what she wanted to see, and all three studied the screen as she began to swipe back and forth, comparing the images. "If this is the 3-D version, I think we are here, on this second level," she said. "That's the garage we started from, and there are more levels above us."

"Does it show any sort of exit?" Tom asked.

"Maybe that's what these are?" she replied, pointing. "I only see three symbols like this."

"Could these lines be ventilation shafts like the one we came in through?" Jason asked.

"That makes sense," Tom said, beginning to see the shape of the maze emerge.

"I wonder why it's so spread out like this, like a giant web? Why not just one big complex?" Ashley asked.

"Maybe so that won't disturb the integrity of the mountain," Jason suggested. "If they honeycombed too much of it, it could collapse."

"That's a scary thought, when you're this far underground," Ashley said with a shiver. "That's another reason I'd like to get out of here."

"OK, what's next?" Jason asked.

"Give me another boost up to those buttons" Ashley suggested. "Let's see what they do."

Once again Jason stooped to boost Ashley, who balanced on his broad shoulders as he straightened, lifting her within range of the row of discs. She reached and touched one but got no reaction. She leaned and touched another, and to their surprise, a door opened in the wall behind them.

"Madam, your chariot awaits you," Jason said, lowering her back to the ground.

"What is that, an elevator?" she asked.

"It sure looks like one," he replied. "It makes sense that they would have something faster to get around than these long corridors."

"But where will it take us?" she asked, stepping toward the open door.

"It's like 'Through the Looking Glass,' my dear," Jason answered. "We go down the rabbit hole and see what awaits us."

Chapter Twenty-three

ANNA AND SARAH RODE AS SWIFTLY as their horses could manage, following the obvious but indirect trail that had been broken by Jason's horse only a few hours earlier. The dramatic colors of the cliffs were a sharp contrast to the stark whiteness of the snow around them. The afternoon sun had burned through the clouds, and its full glare was in their faces as they rode west.

Eventually the tracks they followed merged into the half-covered trail broken by the snowcat during the storm, and now it offered the path of least resistance. Both women realized that they were heading back toward the scene of last evening's accident.

Anna pulled to a halt. "The trail splits here," she said. "The snowcat came from that direction last night," she said, pointing. "If you look closely here, you can even see the tracks Tom and Jason left following us home. But there," she said, pointing to her right "is where the fresher tracks suddenly veer north, toward the cliffs. It's pretty churned up, but it looks like several horses passed that way. I'm guessing that was the way everyone went last night and this morning."

126

"Then we should follow them, right?" Sarah asked.

"Four men went up, but none came down again." Anna noted. "I don't want you to ride into the same trap that they must have encountered."

"Or you either," Sarah said. "Still, unless we go that way, we're just wasting time out here, aren't we?"

Anna stopped and turned toward her. "Sweetie, if I put you in danger out here today, I'll never forgive myself. I nearly lost you last night, and this morning. I've promised myself that it will never happen again. I have to be the worst mother on earth."

"I love you, Mom, but I shouldn't have to remind you that I'm an adult now," Sarah replied. "I can choose what I do. You aren't responsible for me anymore, and as far as I'm concerned, you've already saved my life twice in less than twenty-four hours. You're the best mother on earth."

Anna paused, and for a moment tears welled in her eyes. "Well, I don't want to have do it again." Anna said.

"You can suggest, but I'll decide" Sarah said. "This is an extraordinary situation. People are missing in a storm. People we love. They could be freezing to death."

Anna found no words for a moment, realizing that what she said was probably truer than she knew. Yes, love was the word for it. For Tom especially, she realized, but also for Jason and Ashley, and even Mosely and Chuck. She found the plain-talking cowboys charming, and heroic. She couldn't let any of them down.

"We have to work at finding them. All of us," Sarah added.

"You're right, Sarah," Anna admitted. "We need to move it. We need to do whatever we can to bring them home. Let's go!"

She spurred her horse and began to head north toward the cliffs, but Sarah called to her to stop after only fifty feet.

"What are these odd tracks here?" Sarah asked, pointing to parallel rows of scores of imprints.

Anna nudged her horse and rode a short way back down the trail to where Sarah was studying the tracks. As she approached, she immediately recognized the signs. The moment of truth had arrived. If Sarah was willing to risk her life, she could no longer hide the facts from her.

"Those, honey, are from what you faced last night," Anna told her. "It's probably alien. Tom and Jason know about it. Mosely's almost come face to face with it. We hadn't seen a sign of it since April. I thought it would be safe to bring you here for a visit. Now, two days in, and this is the most dangerous place I can think of."

"Wait. Did you say alien?" Sarah asked. "You mean, a real alien, like from another planet?"

"That's possible," Anna said. "We can't be sure, but that's what we've been…told."

"Told by who?" Sarah asked.

"Well, a sort of…computer, an artificial intelligence. It communicated with us. It led me to you on the trail last night."

"OK, now I'm confused. It led you? Is it alive, or a machine?"

"There's both, honey. It's a crazy world that just got a lot crazier. Sometimes I have to pinch myself, too. Look, all I can say is this is all true, and those tracks were probably from the thing you shot last night. It followed you to the house, I think."

"That thing didn't look much like a bear," Sarah admitted, "but it's crazy to think I just shot an alien. What if I've started an inter-planetary war?"

"I don't think it will come to that, but we have to be extraordinarily careful. These things are smart, and they have weapons."

Sarah patted the rifle strapped to her horse. "So do we," she said. "Let's go."

Chapter Twenty-four

"SEEMS TO ME WE DON'T HAVE that many options," Tom said, looking at the open door of what appeared to be a huge elevator car. "It sure beats running from these beasts. We'll just have to be ready when the door opens in case we're facing another pack of them."

At that thought the three hesitated, but then gingerly stepped into the opening. The door swiftly shut behind them, and the car began to move, not up or down, as expected, but with growing speed sideways.

"What do you suppose this is about," Tom asked, as they braced themselves against the wall.

"I don't know, but let's sit down, in case we come to a sudden stop," Jason replied.

In less than thirty seconds the car began to decelerate, and came to a halt, the door opening with a faint swoosh. Yet another large 'control room' with an array of anterooms greeted them outside the door. As before, a row of panels and buttons lined one wall.

"I think the buttons call a destination," Ashley said. "I see nine of these orange-colored nodes on the chart. I think they're the transportation nodes. If this chart is in 3-D, then there are at least three of these rooms on each level, and five levels. The top and bottom levels don't seem to have these nodes. They're a marked in green, like the other ones we went through that were just dormitories or something. This one could be that farm we saw."

"That's progress, then," Jason replied. "See any that are close to exits?"

"Do you think that's one?" Ashley said, pointing at one corridor that seemed to end abruptly.

"It could be," Jason said. "It's one level up, and to the right. That could be the place we found when we were trying to follow your trail. There's a stone door at the entrance, inside a cave. That could be their regular path to get to the ranch."

"And our cattle," Tom added.

"But how do we know which button to push to get there?" Jason asked. "They aren't labeled."

"I think there may be a pattern, but I'm not sure yet. Can we experiment some more?" Ashley asked.

"Nothing better to do," Tom said dryly. "Let's just jump around this place until we find a way out. At least it will keep those creatures off our trail."

Within a minute the car came to a halt and the door slid open.

"Well, that didn't work," Tom said as he gazed at the lighted panel in yet another node of the underground maze. "I think we're back where we started."

"How can you be sure, Dad?" Jason asked after they cautiously stepped into the room. "These nodes are identical, if they aren't all the same place. That could be a different shaft than we saw before."

"Well, let's eliminate that possibility," Tom replied. "Got a pencil or a pen?"

"No, but I have my knife. Let me start numbering these places. We must have passed through six, but I'm not sure if they were six different ones, I'm so turned around."

"This one seems to be in the center of the bottom row, so mark it number one dash two," Tom said, and Jason promptly scratched the number on the wall under the row of panels.

"We still haven't figured out how these buttons work because the arrangement seems to be different at each station, or node, if that's what you want to call them," Ashley observed. She stood studying the pattern on the display and comparing it to the single row of buttons above. "There must be some sort of logical pattern, though," she added. "It can't just be random since there're no marks on the various buttons. I was sure that last one would take us up to the top level, and we went sideways again."

Just then Jason waved his hand for silence and pointed to his left. All three strained their ears and heard a distant sound. It sounded almost like a distant human voice. "Did you hear that?" Jason asked. "It sounded like it came through the shaft."

"I think so too," Tom replied. "let's check it out."

All three stood at the edge of the abyss, which seemed to stretch to infinity in the darkness above and below them. They listened but heard nothing else.

"Let's try giving a call back," Tom suggested. "I don't know what anyone up there can do to help us, but at least they will know that we're down here."

All three joined their voices to shout together. They waited only a moment before hearing a response from below, a strange, multi-syllabic sort of howl. They quickly retreated from the edge.

"OK, that might not have been beneficial," Ashley said, "but it was worth a try. Now let's see if we can figure out how to use these controls again." She was already studying the board again, comparing what she had gleaned from their previous two shuttle rides. "Some of these must be up and down. It stands to reason that they don't just go sideways."

"I think you need to pick one pretty fast," Tom offered, "because there's something coming."

An instant later the recognizable pattering of the footfalls of the predators announced their approach to all.

"Quick, Jason, we need to use those!" Ashley said, pointing.

Jason swiftly ducked to his now-familiar crouch, and she hopped onto his shoulders. He slowly straightened his legs, and she stretched to reach her mark. Seconds later they had ducked into another car, and the door closed behind them. This time, to their relief, they began to rise. In only ten seconds' time they halted, and the men drew their guns as the door automatically slid open. Cautiously they peeked out and saw nothing.

"Let's check out the board here, and see what we've done," Ashley said. They stepped out of the car and into the room, and Ashley immediately turned her attention to the lighted boards. "It seems that we've been able to reach…" she began, before being interrupted by a shout.

"Duck," Jason shouted, and as she reflexively dropped to her knees a shot rang out, and a glowing scimitar clashed against the wall just above her. She turned her head to see the monstrous apparition that had apparently lurked around the curved wall out of sight. Now it stood, apparently dazed by a shot Jason had landed squarely in the center of its body. As Ashley looked, horrified, she realized that there was a small oozing hole right between rows of what appeared to be…eyes that seemed to circle around its trunk. It raised its eyeless head and howled, then staggered backwards, leaving the scimitar behind.

Without thinking, Ashley picked it up. It was surprisingly light, she thought, but it had to be deadly. She aimed the pointed end of it at the beast, but it didn't seem to notice. It was in the process of curling up against the wall behind it, settling into a heap and wrapping its arms and legs around its body like a blanket. Ashley thought it looked even more like a gigantic spider, except for the vicious-looking jaws that remained protruding and waving on a long neck at the top of the folded creature.

"That's one out of the fight," Tom said.

"I don't think they've encountered anything like guns before," Jason said. "They've been dealing with big horn sheep and deer as prey, most likely, and haven't had to face another intelligent species."

"It was waiting here to ambush us, like some sort of samurai."

"Remember, they're intelligent," Jason said. "They must have figured out that we're using these shuttles to evade them."

"If that's the case, we may need to change tactics again," Tom said.

Ashley looked at the strange weapon she had taken from the beast. Three feet of handle led to another six feet of blade. The edge of the blade seemed to have some sort of electric charge and glowed with a faint light, but the tip was blunt. Immediately she raised it over her head and touched a button. Nothing happened. She poked another in the row. A door opened behind them. "Let's go," she said.

The trio dashed through the doors and in moments it began to rise.

"These things are life-savers, so far," Tom said as they were swept swiftly upward. "I wonder why these creatures don't just use them too?

"Maybe they're afraid of them, like they were that street-sweeper," Ashley suggested, "or maybe they're superstitious. Most primitive cultures were. They may consider them deities, some sort of gods or something, or even haunted chambers."

"This is all haunted chambers, as far as I'm concerned," Jason said, as the door opened to another of the identical control rooms. They carefully exited, and Tom and Jason split to peer around the curved central wall to be sure there wasn't another ambush planned. All seemed clear.

"Let's call this room two-three," Ashley said, again sweeping her hand across the display board. Jason promptly withdrew his knife and scratched the numbers on the face of the metal.

"I'm beginning to see the pattern, I think" Ashley said. "It will probably seem easy once I figure it out. It's apparent that these were built by, and for, the original colonists. What's got me puzzled is, why are they still running, and what powers them?"

"As long as it's helping us stay ahead of those things, I don't care. I'm just happy it all works," Jason said.

"Right now, the lack of water is as big a problem as these creatures are," Tom said. "My canteen's almost empty, and I'm pretty parched, so I know both of you are, too. I'm not saying we should stop trying to find our way out, but we need to keep thinking about water. Don't you imagine these creatures need some, too? Or do they drink something else?"

Ashley shuddered at the thought. "Let's not even think about that. Let's just find our way home. I've got a life I'd like to live."

"Then let's get to work," Jason said. "Those things are not likely to leave us alone for long without trying some new attack. You've made some progress interpreting these panels, and I don't think I learned anything about them from that sphere, so why don't you just keep going."

As Ashley continued to study the glowing holographic panel that seemed to guide them, Tom and Jason took up positions to guard the entrances to the room. There was one connecting tunnel, that presumably went to another node, and two ramps, which led to higher and lower levels of the complex. So long as they were covered, they figured, Ashley should have all the time she needed to plot their course out of the maze.

'Somehow there's a pattern here,' Ashley told herself. 'These circles have to correspond to these nodes…' As she scrolled through the various displays, it seemed that she counted only three shafts and three levels, making nine of the nodes they had identified as the 'control' rooms, though what they controlled remained a mystery. 'But what if…' she thought, 'they aren't really control rooms at all? What if the buttons are only…' Suddenly she had an idea. Taking her new weapon, she again touched just the tip of it to one of the buttons. Nothing happened. She tried a second button. A port opened, revealing another of the transport cars.

"Are we leaving?" Jason asked, seeing the open door.

"Not yet, I'm trying to test a theory," Ashley told him.

After a short wait, Ashley again reached with her weapon and made contact with two other buttons in succession. The same door opened. She reached into the pocket of her jeans and found an old shopping list. She tossed it into the car and waited. Again, the door closed.

Returning to the controls, she touched a third pair of buttons. The door opened, and the same car was there. Her scrap of paper was still on the floor.

"I think it senses when it's empty and won't move," she called to the two men, turning away from the panel. "It seems that the buttons aren't like a simple lift because it goes up, down, and sideways. The buttons call up coordinates. They have codes just like we've started scratching on the walls. It takes two buttons to call up a destination. So, if we can match the destinations to..." "Ashley!" Jason screamed, and she threw herself to the side, hitting the ground as Jason fired his gun. One of the beasts had sprung from the darkness of the shaft itself and headed straight toward Ashley. Jason's shot only seemed to glance off the curve of its body, but it hesitated just long enough for Ashley to roll to the wall and kneel pointing the scimitar toward the attacker. The beast stopped, and swiftly retreated into the hole.

By the time Tom had dashed from the opposite side of the room the battle had been won. The entire attack had lasted only seconds.

"Did you hit it?" Tom asked, helping Ashley up from the floor still clutching her scimitar.

"I don't think it had any effect," Jason replied. "It was Ashley's sword that stopped it."

"Why didn't you shoot it again?" Tom asked.

"I would have, but I was afraid that it could ricochet and hit Ashley. My first shot seemed to bounce off, like it was wearing armor."

"That's not good. We got little enough ammunition as it is," Tom said. "I hope we don't waste it."

"Strange that it didn't seem to recognize guns, but it ran when it saw that I had this sword thing," Ashley said.

"I think it just climbed right up the walls of the shaft, just like we watched it on the slickrock yesterday morning...or the day before," Jason said. "I have no idea how long we have been down here."

"My ears are still ringing from the gunshot," Ashley said, "so it might be my imagination, but I think I just heard someone calling."

The three gathered as near the shaft edge as they dared and listened in silence. For a moment Jason thought he heard the faint sound of squishy footfalls, but they quickly faded. Then a loud crack and the distinct sound of a ricochet echoed down the shaft from above. Jason waved the others to silence. Moments later, he heard the faint metallic clink of a spent bullet from the pit far below.

Chapter Twenty-Five

F RUSTRATED BY THEIR INABILITY TO GO any further or locate the missing trio, Chuck and Mosely turned and began the long walk back toward the tunnel's entrance. They had gone only a hundred feet or so when Mosely suddenly stopped. "Chuck, did you hear that?

"Hear what?"

"Come back here," Mosely said. "I think I just heard a gunshot. It sounded like a Colt, and that's what Tom and Jason carry. They could be signaling us."

Mosely was already hurrying back toward the shaft, with Chuck following behind. When he reached it, he quickly dropped to the ground and hung his head over the abyss. He heard…something. Was that a voice? "Hallooo…" he shouted.

No response came.

Mosely pulled out his revolver, and aimed into the darkness, pointing the gun slightly downward and to the right. He fired a round and heard it ricochet counterclockwise around the walls, pinging sharply before its energy was spent. As the ringing of his own shot faded, he listened for any sort of response.

Below, the stranded group couldn't help but hear. "That was a shot," Jason told the others.

"Yeah, no doubt," Tom said, stepping closer to the edge. "Helllooooo!" he shouted up the shaft.

"Halloo!" came an answering echo from above. Jason cautiously approached the sheer drop, casting his light about the opening, checking for an ambush. It seemed clear. Gathering his courage, he lay on his back and stuck his head over the ledge, looking up. "It's Jason!" he shouted.

A moment later, he heard the faint but familiar voice of Mosely, shouting back. "We come to get ya' out!"

•

Anna and Sarah rode carefully up the lower part of the talus slope following the trail left by the others. "Let's dismount here," Anna suggested. "It's too dangerous for the horses. We'll have to walk the rest of the way. Bring the lights."

"You seem to know where we're going," Sarah observed. "I would never have thought to bring lights in the first place. Want to fill me in?"

"There's a tunnel up here, Sarah. It goes straight into the mountain for more than a quarter mile and ends at a shaft. I went in there before, last year, with Jason. That may be where these things live."

"OK, so now we're heading into the lion's den…" she replied.

"If you've changed your mind about doing this, that's fine, sugar. I'd rather you didn't come along any farther."

"Are you kidding me?" Sarah replied with a nervous laugh as she slung her rifle over her shoulder. "Really, I love this stuff. No, I'm definitely going with you. After all, you're my only mother, too."

"Can you make it up the slope with that rifle, Sarah?" Anna asked. "I don't think I can manage to carry mine,

Together they struggled up the loose, slippery slope, an icy breeze on their faces, their gloved hands and booted feet digging into the foot-deep snow to find traction in the rocks beneath. Their efforts were enough to keep them warm, even though the late afternoon had grown still colder as the sun had descended.

"Is that the tunnel?" Sarah said at last as she paused to catch her breath. "The tracks lead straight to it."

Anna looked to where Sarah pointed. "That's it. Now we have to climb up that rope."

"Well, that looks easy," Sarah deadpanned. "Climb up this thread, and come into my lair, said the spider."

"You may not be far from the truth there," Anna answered, "based upon what I've been told."

At last they reached the rope dangling down the face of the rock. "I'll go first," Sarah said. "I think I can do this." She slung her rifle over her shoulder and tugged on the rope.

"Use your feet on the rock, and hands on the rope." Anna told her. "You have to sort of walk up, a bit at a time."

"I sure am glad for the volleyball training now!" Sarah replied, swiftly pulling herself up the rock face. In a minute she had reached the tunnel entrance, and immediately shone her light into the dark interior. "It's empty," she called down.

Anna tied her saddlebag to the rope. "Here, pull this up," she said. Moments later the line dropped back down. Anna grasped it and began to struggle up the mountain. 'I guess I'm not in as good a shape as my daughter,' she thought. 'No surprise there!'

"Mom, please hurry," Sarah said. "There's something coming."

"Don't let it get close to you, Sarah. Shoot it if you have to."

"It's not me, Mom. It's heading toward you!"

Startled, Anna looked around. Only a few hundred feet away, something was approaching across the face of the slickrock. Anna willed herself to be strong, and the instant shot of adrenaline helped. In seconds she scrambled alongside her daughter.

"What is that thing?" Sarah asked, horrified as she watched the approach of the yellowish creature.

"Let's just go!" Anna said. "Quick, deeper into the tunnel."

Sarah led the way, the bright beam illuminating the interior of the tunnel. Anna carried her saddlebag as she ran. The daylight behind suddenly dimmed, and she glanced over her shoulder. The creature was at the tunnel entrance.

Chapter Twenty-Six

"WHAT CAN WE DO TO HELP YOU?" Chuck hollered into the black depths of the shaft.

A moment passed before a faint shout came back to his ears. "We need water!"

"That was Tom's voice," Chuck said. "So at least they're both OK. We don't know about Ashley, though."

"Let's ask them," Mosely suggested. "Is Miss Ashley with you?" he called.

"Mosely!" came a feminine shout from below. "Be careful! Don't come down here! Those things live here!"

"Well, that's something, then," Mosely said. "They need water, and if they're down there with those things, they probably need ammunition, too!"

"I've got a canteen, but how on earth would I get it down to them?"

"Didn't you notice the cord that was strung down the tunnel?" Mosely replied. "It seemed to go on and on, but it ended a couple hundred feet back."

Chuck turned toward the tunnel entrance, then paused. "Hey, Mose, what time is it?"

"Why do you want to know that?" Mosely asked, glancing at his watch. "It's 4:10."

"Then the sun's still up, so I think we got a visitor, or maybe more than one," Chuck replied. "The light's flickering like a firefly."

Mosely turned toward the tunnel and saw that the tiny disc of light that had been visible in the inky blackness was now dimmed.

"And whatever has gotten into the tunnel is heading this way, I think," Chuck added.

Suddenly the light flashed bright, then faded again. "That's some sort of flashlight, being aimed down the tunnel," Mosely said. "Maybe it's the Sheriff's men."

"That would be great," Chuck said. "We could use some help."

"Halloo!" Mosely called back down the tunnel.

"Mosely!" called a distant feminine voice. "There's something following us!"

"Keep coming!" he called, and immediately began to run toward the women.

Chuck turned back toward the open shaft. "We're sending down water!" he called. "Give us a couple of minutes."

"Please hurry!" came an answering call from the depths.

In a minute Mosely reached the women in the depths of the tunnel. "Quick, Chuck's just ahead, and we've been talking to the others," he told them. Behind them he could see the scuttling creature that was pursuing them. "Oh, and grab that cord, and pull it along with you," He added. "I'll see if I can stop this thing."

Anna looked down and saw the thin cord and recognized it as the one that Jason had measured out a year earlier. She picked it up and continued running. Mosely aimed his revolver carefully down the tunnel and fired off a shot. In the confines the shot was almost deafening, but the beast behind hesitated only a moment. It seemed to be crawling on all-fours. 'Or all eights,' Mosely thought to himself. 'That is one ugly critter!'

He fired off another shot, and was sure he had struck the beast, now closing to only a couple hundred feet, but it kept coming. Mosely thought he could see a faint arc of light waving in front of it. He turned and ran.

"It's still coming. It was almost like my shots bounced off it," he told the others. Chuck was busily tying the canteen to the end of the cord, and dropped it over the edge, playing out the line as it descended.

"Here, try my rifle!" Sarah said, unslinging the weapon and handing it to Mosely. Remembering the noise of his earlier shots, he grabbed the gun and ran away from the others, straight at the approaching beast. When he got within fifty feet, he aimed dead center and fired. It kept coming. He tried again, and this time he got a reaction. The beast gave a strange howl, and stopped, scuttling backwards a few feet. Mosely waited to see what it would do. 'No sense in using up the ammunition if there's more than a couple of these things,' he told himself.

When the beast didn't move any further, Mosely began to back away, returning to his friends. He found them huddled near the edge of the shaft, still lowering the canteen.

"I stopped it for now," Mosely reported. "I don't know if I killed it, though, so we need to be on guard."

Sarah turned the floodlight down the tunnel. She could see nothing within the reach of the beam. "It's clear for now," she reassured them.

"That cord's been lying in this tunnel since last year, and it could be rotten," Anna said. "I just hope it's strong enough to hold all the way down."

"So far, so good," Chuck said.

"Hey, what's that sound?" Sarah asked.

Everyone fell silent for a moment.

"I can't hear anything," Mosely whispered. "My ears are still ringing."

"Well, I hear something," Sarah said. "It sounds…squishy, like walking in mud."

"There's something climbing the wall," Anna said. "They're coming up here."

•

Ashley stood near the precipice with Tom next to her, his ears tuned for any sound from the shaft, his revolver at the ready. Jason had stepped away and was guarding the approaches. "I hope they hurry with the water," Ashley said. "Those things could come back at any moment."

Moments later they heard a faint scraping on the wall of the shaft just above their heads. Tom crouched and aimed. Ashley stepped back and listened. It repeated, getting quickly closer.

"That doesn't sound like a creature," she said. "That could be the canteen."

She flicked on their floodlight, and saw the canteen sliding down the wall nearby. "It's out of reach," she said, as it slid past them and continued into the depths.

"Stop!" Tom called. "Give us a minute to reach it!"

No answer came from above. Had they been heard? Ashley had already found her captured weapon, and reached it into the shaft, trying to extend it to touch the dangling cord. A sudden echo of a gunshot made her hesitate. A moment later, there was another.

"I don't think they are signaling us," Ashley said. They may be in trouble."

"They've gone to a lot of effort to send us water," Tom cautioned. "Just be careful, and don't cut the cord!"

"I need to use the back of the thing, but it curves the wrong way," Ashley said. "Maybe if I can just get it to swing away from the wall, it might come this way. They've got it on hundreds of feet of line, so it's going to be springy…"

On her third attempt she managed to give the line a solid nudge. It seemed to hesitate as the weight of the canteen reacted, then swung slowly back in their direction, scraping against the wall. Tom sat down, held Ashley's hand, and she leaned into the shaft to retrieve it. At last it played across her fingers, and in seconds they had raised the full canteen.

"Thank goodness!" Ashley said.

"That's enough to hold us, hopefully, until we can find our way out of this place," Tom said, offering it first to Ashley. She raised it to her lips as another distant shot echoed down the shaft. "Sounds like they've run into some trouble up there," Tom added. "I wish we could help."

"I think there's something coming," Jason called. "Let's move on."

•

"It looks like we're going to have to fight our way back out of here," Mosely said, as the group retreated from the edge of the shaft.

"At least we got them some water, and gave them a fighting chance," Chuck observed grimly. "That's what we've got, too, so let's take it to 'em."

"We can't tell how many are coming up the walls, but we can't escape that direction, anyway, and as far as we know, there's only one blocking the tunnel," Anna pointed out.

"But it's a wounded animal, so there's no telling what it might do," Mosely said. "I'm pretty sure I got it with that second rifle shot. It pulled up short. I wasn't far away."

Sarah had been looking back toward the shaft, and suddenly screamed. Anna whipped the light back in that direction and saw the terrible sight of ten-foot-long arms stretching into the tunnel. The bulky body of the creature, topped by the fearsome jaws, was trying to force its way into the narrow space.

Chuck raised his revolver, and an ear-shattering crack sent a bullet directly into the creature's open jaws. It gave a short howl and quickly retreated. "We can probably hold them off for a good while, but we don't know how many there are," he said. "The tunnel seems a bit small for them to get through easily, so that's something in our favor, but I'm all for getting out of this tunnel, and facing these things in the open."

"Then let's go," Mosely said, and began to stride toward the beast that still crouched in the tunnel, blocking their escape.

Anna alternated directions with the light, checking first ahead and then behind, watching for pursuit. In moments they were approaching the wounded creature. Its sprawling legs and the bulk of its body nearly blocked the tunnel. It raised its head and made a strange snorting sound.

"Maybe it's a good thing you didn't kill it, Mose," Chuck said. "Unless we can get that thing to retreat, we may be stuck. I don't know if we could fit past it."

"Well, how are we going to get it to retreat?" Mose said. "If I shoot it again, it's liable to die right there. I sure don't want to try to crawl over it, not with those jaws, they're liable to chomp on me, and not to even mention those arms and legs. That thing looks strong. And it ran off with all that beef before, so I know it is."

"Listen, guys, we need to come up with an idea soon, because whatever's behind us is likely to try again, and we can't just stay here," Anna said. "We came up here to try to help you, not just get stuck with you."

"Got any suggestions?" Chuck said. "I think I'm fresh out, at the moment."

"How about fire?" Sarah suggested. "Most animals are afraid of fire."

"Good idea," Chuck said, "but we've got nothing to burn."

"How about this?" Sarah replied, holding up part of the cord that still trailed across the tunnel floor. "It's just some sort of heavy twine."

"Most of that we lowered down the hole," Mosely said, "but we might be able to pull some of it back up." He began tugging on the cord and had soon gathered several handfuls.

"Can we make a torch with it?" Anna asked. "We don't really have anything to put it on to hold it."

"Can we use the rifle barrel?" Sarah suggested.

"As long as you don't get it too hot and warp the barrel," Chuck offered.

"I'd trade a rifle for a way out of here," Mosely said. "We still got our revolvers if we need to shoot something."

"OK, then, let's try it," Anna said, and began to quickly wind the cord around the end of the gun barrel.

"Does this stuff even burn?" Chuck asked.

"Let me test a piece of it," Mosely replied. He pulled his knife and cut a six-inch piece of the cord, held it up, and struck a match. The flame quickly danced up the length of twine, emitting a puff of smoke.

"Hey, did you see that?" Anna asked. "The smoke blew back toward the shaft. I think this plan might have a double purpose. The smoke might help discourage the ones behind us, too." She swiftly finished wrapping a lump of cord the size of a tennis ball around the end of the barrel. "No sense in waiting," she said. "It's time to try this thing out."

Mosely took the rifle from Anna and began to lead the group forward toward the huge creature blocking the tunnel. He advanced to within twenty feet, and paused, keeping the rifle aimed at it. "Got a light?" he asked.

Chuck struck another match and touched it to the knot of fibers. A bright flame immediately leapt from it, and a dense stream of smoke swept through the clustered group.

"Hold your breath!" Anna said.

Mosely advanced toward the beast holding the flaming torch, and it seemed to glow in the firelight. The jaws that faced them were opening and closing slowly, but the trunk of the beast lay on its side. There were rows of openings around the trunk, and upper side seemed to be opening as well. Above and below those rows the beast appeared to be wearing some sort of metallic armor.

With a sudden snuffing sound, the predator lurched away from the flame in a sort of wave motion, wriggling backwards toward the opening. Mosely advanced, and again it retreated, and this time maintained a sort of intermittent retreat.

Sarah briefly cast the floodlight back toward the shaft again and saw no sign of pursuit. "It's working!" she said.

Moments later, the torch began to burn out.

"Um, got any more of that string?" Mosely asked.

Chapter Twenty-Seven

ASHLEY'S CHOICE OF BUTTONS had again been correct, because the car they entered again rose. "At least we know now that this is the shaft we came in through, and sort of have our bearings within the maze," Jason said as they were whisked upward.

"I've still got no clue about east or west," Tom observed, "but I can tell up from down. Up seems better to me," he added with a wry smile.

"Well, so far you've done well," Ashley said. "You've shot up a few of these creatures, and we're all still here."

"You're the one who's done well," Tom said. "I couldn't have figured out those charts and buttons if my life depended upon it."

"It still may," Jason spoke up, "so let's not get cocky. We're not out of here yet."

"Listen to this young man, scolding his father!" Tom said in mock horror. "What's this younger generation coming to?"

"Thanks for keeping it light, Tom," Ashley said, giving Jason a sidelong glance. "We're all under enough stress already."

The car suddenly halted, and they crept out, guns at the ready. As before, the room seemed clear. "Hey, this is a place we never found before!" Tom said, glancing around.

Jason and Ashley looked around the room at a complex array of panels and devices mounted high on the walls. Before each one there were what appeared to be some sort of tables, about five feet high. There were also mechanical-looking controls with wide flaps for handles.

"What do you suppose this is?" Tom asked.

"I think we may have finally found the actual 'control room' of this place," Ashley replied. "Those other nodes were just transport hubs, I guess. I had noticed on the chart before that there was only one node with two rings of color, orange and purple, so I thought it might be unique.

"Well, I can't say much for the decorator colors, but I'm glad you picked this place, Ashley," Jason said. "Maybe we can get the upper hand on these things from here." All three began to study the panels, Ashley boldly standing atop the tables, touching and swiping the screens to see what they displayed.

"I just realized that these probably aren't tables," Jason said. "They come up to my chest, but for those beasts, they're probably benches."

Ashley looked down at the surface she was standing on. "You're probably right, but I wonder about the beings that built all this. They were sized for them, after all, so they must have been large, too. Were they peaceful? Humanoid? Were these things attacking us just docile pets to them? Why did they disappear? Was there some sort of plague?"

"Good question," Jason said. "If they were dying and knew it, would they leave some sort of message behind? I think I would, if the situation were reversed and I was the last survivor on some alien planet."

Ashley turned back to the panel. "Maybe that's what the sphere was. It might have been a last signal to whoever found them."

"The Messenger was certainly one of their tools, and seemed to know a great deal about humans, too," Jason said. "Maybe it was intelligent enough to run this place, to keep the lights and machinery up and running."

"If that's the case, did these predators sign their own death warrant when they destroyed it?" Tom asked.

"There's definitely some things that aren't yet clear to me," Jason said. "Even though that sphere was sharing information, it didn't include every detail."

"Understanding all this is great, but my focus is going to remain on getting out of this place," Tom said. "Those things mean business, and we are really low on ammunition."

"So how will we ever escape?" Ashley asked. "Without food and water, we can only last so long. I'm famished now."

Jason dug into his pack and pulled out an energy bar. "Here, it's the last one. I was saving it until you spoke," he told Ashley. "This will help a bit."

"I'm not eating that unless we split it three ways," Ashley told him. "You guys need to keep up your strength as much, no, more than I do."

"OK, have it your way, Ashley, but take another sip of water, too," Jason replied. "Here's a third of the bar," he said, handing her a portion. She ate it ravenously.

Jason stepped up on one of the tables and approached a panel. "I'd like to think that this place was set up to run itself, but who knows." He reached out his hand to touch the screen, and it lighted in reaction, but then a strange thing happened. A brighter light seemed to pour out of it, and Jason was enveloped in a strange, static glow.

Jason didn't move but stared at the screen for several long seconds. Tom dashed from his place near the entrance to stand at his feet, looking up at his son, his face a mask of fear. Then the light suddenly faded, and Jason stood transfixed for a moment. Then he looked down at his father. "That was interesting." he said.

●

Mosely was letting the beast have no peace. Having wounded it once, and approached it with the fire, it seemed to want no part of him, and continued to back away every time he got close. He had retrieved the long-bladed sword it had left behind, and it seemed to fear the glowing blade as much as it had the torch.

Anna kept a watch behind, worried that once the smoke cleared the tunnel the rest might resume the attack. Sarah busied herself reeling in as much of the twine as she was able to drag down the long corridor, slowly rebuilding the torch, in case it was needed.

It took almost half an hour before the beast backed all the way to the tunnel opening, and it seemed to slither out and down the cliff face. "I think it's hurt pretty bad," Chuck said. "It probably won't be giving us any more trouble."

"You may be right, Chuck," Mosely replied, "but let's just hope he doesn't have a few buddies around looking for revenge."

When the foursome reached the opening, they looked out into a starry night. Icy air filled their lungs, but it felt good. There was already no sign of the beast they had followed, and their rope still dangled near the opening. "Nothing to do now but head back and see if we can get more help," Chuck said.

"We'd need a few hundred feet of rope to reach down to where they were trapped, and lots of muscle to pull them back up," Mosely said, grasping the rope to slip back down the face of the rock.

"Jason keeps lots of rope in the barn," Anna said. "He's into rock climbing. I've seen coils of it hanging there. I wish now that I'd brought them, but I didn't know that we'd end up needing it."

One by one they lowered themselves down the face of the rock until they were gathered at the top of the steep trail. They started moving carefully down the slope, Mosely in the lead. Chuck carried the light, trying to illuminate the way forward, while also keeping a watch all around from behind. A quarter moon hung in a windless sky to their west.

It took twenty minutes to return to where they had left the horses. "Oh, my god," Anna said when she stepped next to Mosely, who was already examining the scene. Large pieces of horse were strewn across the ground.

"Looks like they got Two-bit," Mosely said. "Dang, he was a good horse. In fact, he was the best damn quarter horse around, probably in the whole Four Corners. Damned aliens! Now they got me pissed off!"

"I don't see any sign of the other horses," Chuck said when he had descended the last few feet and stood with the others. He cast his light in a large circle around the area and saw nothing but a snowy landscape that had been churned by the horses, and the predators, into a bloody mess.

"Can we just go on?" Sarah said. "I don't mind walking, I just don't want to stand here in the middle of all this."

"Sure, we don't have any other choice now, all the other horses probably ran off, and they're likely waiting for us back at the barns. I don't blame them at all, after what happened to Two-bit." Mosely said, but then paused. "I wonder if the cell service ever came back." He reached into his pocket and drew his out, and the others all fumbles for theirs as well. "I got nothing," he reported.

"Same here," Sarah said.

"Nope," Chuck chimed in. "Let's just get moving. The more distance we put between us and those critters the better I'm gonna' feel."

The group set out across the ranch, the glow of the moon casting a light at their backs, enough to illuminate the obvious trail that had been broken by the horses the night before and trampled down further by their own approach that morning. In the distance an owl hooted, but otherwise everything was quiet, which only made the crunching of their boots in the snow seem deafening.

"It's a bit too quiet for my liking," Mosely said. "I'd like to be serenaded by some coyotes. Can you make that happen, Chuck?"

Chuck sniffed. "It's not something I'd arrange for just anybody, but let me see what I can do," he said.

"I'm worried about our friends still down in that pit, so I don't even want to think about anything else," Anna said.

Suddenly the silence was broken by an eerie, high-pitched howl that seemed to last for more than ten seconds. "That weren't no coyote," Mosely said.

"No," Chuck agreed. "I think we better be hurrying along. We've still got a few miles to go before we get back to the C9 ranch house."

Above them, unseen, a file of dark shadows was descending the face of the slickrock.

Chapter Twenty-Eight

SARAH HAD HER RIFLE SLUNG OVER HER SHOULDER to make walking easier in the deep snow. Likewise, Mosely and Chuck had holstered their revolvers, but Chuck marched along with his glowing scimitar over his shoulder, proud of the trophy he'd won. "You look like one of the soldiers of the Wicked Witch of the West," Sarah told him. "Maybe you could chant a little. You know, like 'Yo, ho, low-ray-o' or something."

Even Anna laughed a bit nervously at the comparison. "Yeah, you do, Chuck," she told him, "but I don't think the comparison's fair to you. You're much more noble than that bunch."

"Well, I wouldn't mind using this thing on a couple of those critters," Chuck replied. "I wonder what all it does."

"It's obviously more than just a blade," Anna said. "That glowing edge seems to have some sort of charge. Here, why don't you test it out on that old stump there?"

Chuck glanced to where she pointed and saw the remains of a long dead tree poking two feet above the snow. He stepped aside, whipped the blade toward it, and the tree virtually exploded, leaving flames bursting from the shortened stump. Everyone jumped back at the pop, and the sudden burst of flame.

"Dang, it went through like it was soft as butter!" Chuck exclaimed. "What do you suppose made it do that?"

"As I said, it seems to have some sort of charge," Anna said. "I imagine that's what they used to cut up the cattle. And Jason's truck," she added.

"And poor old Two-bit," Mosely chimed in. "Nasty weapon. I wonder if you can turn it on and off? I don't see any sort of switch. Does the battery wear down?"

"I doubt it runs on batteries," Anna said. "These things must have some other sort of energy. Maybe it gets it from an exterior source, through the air, somehow. Or, who knows, maybe it has a compact fission reactor. It's obviously different technology than what we have."

"Well, I still wish I could turn it off, because it's kind of dangerous as it is," Chuck said.

"It just went off," Sarah said. "The light's gone."

"Well, shoot, maybe I spoke too soon, I was hoping to use it on some of those critters, after what they did to Two-bit."

"No problem, it's on again," Sarah pointed out.

Anna stopped walking and looked at Chuck and the scimitar. "Did you just turn it off and back on?" she asked.

"Did I do that?" Chuck said.

"Maybe you did," Anna replied. "Wish it off again."

Chuck looked at the long weapon, and opened his mouth to speak, but it had already turned off. "Well, I'll be danged!" he said.

"May I hold it for a moment?" Anna asked.

"Of course," he replied.

Anna took the weapon from him. In a second or two the blue glow again gleamed along its edge. A second later, it was gone again. "Amazing," said Anna. "It works by the will of the person holding it, even though we are an alien species to its makers."

"I think we'd best be making time," Mosely interjected. "There's something moving out there. Those things are probably planning some sort of surprise party."

Everyone's attention instantly turned from the weapon to the situation, and they moved quickly toward the distant ranch house, staying in a tight group.

Chapter Twenty-Nine

"JASON, ARE YOU ALRIGHT?" Ashley shouted in a panicky voice, anxiously grasping his shoulders and looking in his eyes. She had leapt from table to table to reach him in seconds.

"It's OK, I'm fine," he replied with a smile. "I just got another lesson. It was amazing. Don't be afraid of this, Ashley. It worked just like the sphere. Obviously, this is the actual central brain that sent the Messenger to us. It's an artificial intelligence that communicated with me."

"It's just like what happened before," Tom told her. "It seems these beings, or their robots, communicate with light, somehow."

"The sphere was just a tool. That's why I called it the Messenger. I didn't know who sent it before. Now I do. This is the central brain," Jason said. "Now it's teaching me directly, and what it's telling me is pretty amazing."

"This is all overwhelming, but I'm trying to keep up with you, Jason," Ashley said. "If it's teaching you, and it's friendly, will it call off the attack on us?"

"I don't think it can do that, but it definitely wants to help protect us," he answered.

"But why haven't they already attacked us here? With all these doorways, they could come at us from different directions, and we probably couldn't stop them."

"You will think this is really strange," Jason replied, "but I think they are forbidden. It seemed to tell me that their masters set this up as a pet-free zone. Maybe if they try to enter, they get a shock, like one of those invisible dog fences."

"You're kidding!" Tom said.

"No," Jason said. "Here, I think we're safe, but once we leave this room, they will attack us."

"But we can't just stay here with no food or water," Ashley said.

"Knowledge is our best tool," Jason said. "I thought I had learned a lot before, but it wasn't all quite clear. Now it's beginning to make more sense. For one thing, I believe that the beings who built this refuge, since that's what they called it, weren't just pioneers. They were escaping some sort of disaster. I think their planet was very much Earth-like, but it was in the path of an asteroid or some sort of rogue planetary body. It was doomed. They needed a new place with oxygen in the atmosphere."

"So, they all came here?" Ashley asked. "This place isn't big enough to support a fugitive civilization. What have we seen, perhaps room enough for a few hundred, maybe a thousand?"

"I don't think this was the only refuge," Jason replied. "Maybe it was the only one on our planet, but I got the impression that they sent these colonies to multiple places. They headed to far-flung reaches of the galaxy, looking for habitable worlds to move to. And the colonists here didn't die out, they left. They went to join the others on a planet without another intelligent species, because they didn't want to interfere with us. They understood humans, somehow, maybe even communicated with them. They weren't hostile, they were caring. It seemed to be apologizing and explaining what happened."

"So then, what about these 'pets' they left behind?" Tom asked. "If they were so caring, why did that happen?"

"That was apparently an accident," Jason replied. "They may have thought they had them all, but they missed at least a breeding pair. Maybe a couple of them ran away, and they couldn't account for them all when they left. It took centuries, but they reproduced, and reverted to their wild ways."

"So how long have the others been gone?" Ashley asked.

"Not so long as I imagined before," Jason answered. "I think they arrived maybe two or three thousand years ago, and they may have been here for just a few hundred years."

"Wait, when did the first Puebloan people suddenly vanish?" Tom asked. "Wasn't that around that time? There are pictographs up in Horseshoe Canyon of tall beings that look positively alien, with smaller human figures around them. And there are other shapes, too, like tall spindles, that no one understands."

"That's it!" Jason said. "That's what it was trying to tell me!"

"What?" Ashley asked. "Tell us!"

"I could perceive an image of these beings working alongside humans, as friends," Jason told them. "The thing that had me confused was it didn't seem like it was here on Earth. I got a distinct impression of a blueish sun, so I didn't believe it was a real image, just a piece of propaganda or something, telling us that they were friendly. It could be that it was blue, because it wasn't *our* sun, but another one, far away. It's possible they had friendly relations with local people here, and some of them left with them!"

Ashley almost gasped audibly. "If that's true, there are already humans living on other planets," she said, "in advanced civilizations! You know, a couple of days ago I wouldn't have believed a word you are saying. But now it's suddenly plausible."

"But even if this is all true, it still won't help us escape these feral animals they left behind," Tom said.

"Right!" Ashley said.

"Did it tell you how to get out of here, Jason?" Tom asked. "That's the most important thing to me right now. I want the three of us back at the ranch, and away from these devils."

"In a way, it did, Dad. But if I understood what it was suggesting, it won't be easy.

Jason paused before answering. "This AI understands that the beasts are a danger to us," he said, "and it wants to help us. It basically showed me some options that may work. But first, we'll have to get down to the lowest level."

"But that's where these things hang out!" Ashley asked.

"I'm afraid that's right," Jason answered. "We don't have much choice."

•

The long climb and slog through the snow had taken a toll on the stamina of Anna. "I'm not really cut out for this," she told the others. "Too many class-room hours, study hours, and not enough field work this year."

"I sure am glad we had a good Christmas Eve dinner, and a solid breakfast!" Sarah added. "I'm getting pretty hungry again."

"Was that only yesterday?" Anna asked. "It seems like a week ago."

"Yes, and that nice lunch Juanita fixed up for us was still packed up on my horse," Sarah answered.

"I think we may not be the only hungry things around," Mosely said. "It looks like those things are trying to surround us."

Everyone looked as he shined the light in different directions, indicating where he thought the predators were. "There's definitely one back there," he said, looking behind, "but I think they're planning some sort of trap. We're just slogging along following this snowcat trail, so they can see where we're heading next."

"We need to do something unexpected," Anna said. "Like head back along the cliffs."

Everyone looked to the north, where the setting crescent moon still illuminated the face of the mountains. "Back toward where we came from?" Sarah asked, incredulous.

"Not directly, but better that than walk into a trap," Anna told her. "There's no cover at all out here. We need some terrain, rather than this arena they are putting us in."

"I agree," said Mosely. "I've been holding my fire, because here I can't get a clear shot in the dark, and I don't want to waste ammunition. Let's see if we can take the high ground for a change, and maybe we can pick some of them off. Come on, I'll break a trail through the snow."

Mosely angled to the left toward the talus slope that marked the foot of the cliffs. In minutes they were among a field of boulders and climbing slightly uphill. Chuck took up rearguard position, continually shining the light around. A few times he thought he caught a glimpse of something moving, but never clear enough to waste a bullet on.

"Here, Sarah, why don't you take the light back, and let me use your rifle," Chuck said. "I'm going to try to teach these critters a little respect."

"It's all I've got," Sarah said. "Can I use your gun?"

"Sure, do you think you can handle a .45? It's got a big kick."

"Trust me," Sarah said. "I've fired a gun a few times, and I'll use two hands. Those things aren't getting close to me."

"It won't do much good unless they get up close with that armor they're wearing, so don't fire unless they do," Chuck told her

Anna followed closely behind Mosely, trying to watch both flanks at once, knowing that their every move was being watched by a hostile gang. The question in her mind was, how many? Was it two or three, or fifteen or twenty? In the case of the latter, she wouldn't want to count on their odds.

After five minutes, Mosely began to turn back toward the east and the ranch house, putting the cliffs back on their left, but now a bit closer than before. They trod onward as the moon slid behind the mountains to the west.

"It's getting colder," Sarah said.

"It's to be expected," Mosely told her. "Prob'ly get down to about ten degrees before morning, but I don't plan to spend the night out here. We need to keep moving. We've still got a couple of miles to the house."

"Hey, Mose," Chuck called from the rear of their short procession. "Every time Sarah sweeps the light to the left, I think I see about three of those critters walking alongside us, and they're creeping closer, like they think we can't see 'em. I told Sarah not to focus her light on 'em, but I'm pretty sure that's what they are."

"Do you want to give them a warning, or are you just keeping me informed?" Mosely asked.

"I'm ready to take a shot at them," he replied. "I think they're planning to spring something pretty soon. See anyplace ahead where we can make a stand?"

"It's gotten damned dark out there, but I think I remember a line of boulders just ahead," Mosely said. "Either that's where they're waiting, or it's a spot we could take and use."

Sarah swept the light ahead once more, then stopped. "Hold up, Mosely," she said. "I just saw something up there."

Mosely paused and stared into the moving beam of light. "I can't see much," he said. "Turn it off for a second."

Sarah switched the light off, and the four scanned the close horizon.

"I got two behind us, Mose, I can see the blue from their swords," Chuck said.

"I can see two on our left as well," Anna said. "Those blue lights give them away."

"Well, then, we may have to fight them right here," Mosely said. "I can see five, no, maybe six, just about two hundred feet ahead. It looks like they are going to use those boulders to try to stop us."

All four drew together, forming a tight bunch while they discussed the situation, but keeping their eyes focused outward.

"I think they have us about where they want us," Chuck said. "It's going to be a fight real soon now. Everybody, be careful where you aim, try to hit them right in the middle where their eyes are. There's no armor there. If they get really close, the head is good too."

"I'm scared," Sarah said.

"We're all scared," Anna told her. "Let's just show them that we've got plenty of fight left in us."

Chapter Thirty

"THE ONLY WAY I CAN SEE that we will ever get out of here," Jason told Tom and Ashley, "is to use their own tools and methods. Remember, Ashley, that you asked about why everything here still works? The lights work, that 'streetsweeper' still keeps everything spotlessly clean, the transport system functions, even that big scimitar of yours still has energy?"

"Yeah, who maintains all that?" Tom asked.

"Oddly enough, these animals help do that," Jason told them. "They lived in a sort of symbiotic relationship with the others. They performed tasks for them and were provided for by them. These predators wouldn't have built any of this, but they are smart enough to keep it running, with the help of the computers and probably some robotic equipment that we haven't seen yet. They have access to the power source, which is on the lowest level, essentially in the basement."

"So that explains why the power is still on," Tom acknowledged. "Yeah, I can understand that."

"It seems logical" Jason continued, "that after sending machinery such a long distance to create this outpost and carve these tunnels and chambers in solid rock, that they wouldn't pack it all up again and send it back, especially if there was no home planet to return to. When they evacuated, they just left it behind."

"OK, but how does that help us escape?" Ashley asked.

"More than just the power, and the maintenance," Jason pointed out, "they left the machines that cut these tunnels. If we can't find the exit, then we have to make our own."

"And you think this machinery, whatever it is, will still be working?" Ashley asked him.

"Everything else works, why not that?" Jason asked. "We all rode on the top of that huge sweeper. If the lights still work, and the transport cars, I have no reason to think the boring machine will be any different. They obviously built things to last."

"So, this machine is on the lowest level?" Tom asked.

"My understanding of all this isn't crystal clear, because I don't know how I know," Jason said, "but yes, that's where it has to be. It's almost like an instinctive feeling. I suspect it's a sort of implanted memory."

"But in order to work your plan, we've first got to get past the predators," Tom said. "They seem to have us surrounded in here."

"Well, at least we've got this safe zone right now, to plan our moves," Jason said. "We also have a better command of these lifts. Ashley, have you figured out how these things work well enough to determine if there is a straight shot to the bottom from here?"

"We're on the fourth level, here," Ashley said, pointing at another of the complex 3-D diagrams. "You can see that the lines seem to correspond to these transportation hubs, but there aren't any on the lowest level. I think I can get us straight to the second level, but I don't know how to go down from there, unless there's another one of those ramps."

"We'll have to chance it," Jason said. "Here we're safe from the predators, but we have almost no food or water."

163

Tom grunted his agreement. "Good point," he said. "Then I guess we'd better choose our path carefully. Ashley, can we move laterally as easily down there as we can up here?"

"On the second level, I'd say yes," she answered.

"Then can you see any indication of where ramps might be?" Tom asked.

"Not really, Tom," she replied, "but it seems that they are all connected to the transportation hubs. My question is, do you think we'll be able to start it up if we find it. And how do you direct it? Just point at a rock wall and go forward?"

Neither Jason or Tom responded for a long moment. "Well?" she prompted.

"I think that sometimes you just have to go on faith, and believe that you can make it happen," Jason said. "Something has told me that this is our way out. I want to try it, especially because I don't see any alternative."

"Then I say we go," she said. "Let's try to do this in a way that confuses these predators and leaves them far behind." She studied the board for a long moment. "I think that first we go laterally. That should leave them running across this level. Then down to the second level in one leap, and back to this side again. If we can't find a ramp, at least we might be able to retreat here again."

"If nothing else, we can lead them on a merry chase and wear them out," Jason said.

"Let's do this, then," Tom agreed. "No sense in waiting here."

Chapter Thirty-One

"HERE THEY COME," Chuck said. "there are three of 'em on this side."

"I got two over here," Mosely reported. "Everybody, try to stay about fifteen feet away from each other, no more. If they start swinging those choppers of theirs, we've got to be ready to jump out of the way."

"I'd feel better if we could drop some of them before they get that close," Chuck replied.

"Yeah," Sarah chimed in. "You've got my rifle, or I'd to shoot one right now!"

"Not yet, but on my word," Mosely told them.

"They're getting close!" Anna said.

Mosely glanced around, and could see the shapes of the predators, each with its glowing scimitar. Suddenly the closest one rushed toward them, its weapon poised to strike. The rest followed.

"Now!" Mosely shouted, and the crack of the rifle rang out a split second before the two revolvers held by Mosely and Sarah. Anna used her borrowed .38, thankful that Tom had lent it to her for self-defense. The initial volley stopped four of the attackers, but one of the three charging toward Mosely kept coming, and swung its scimitar at his head. He ducked under the weapon and fired two shots point blank into the center of the beast. It spun crazily, staggered, and raised its scimitar to deliver a downward, chopping blow. Mosely dove to the side and almost escaped, but the blade cut into his leg as it sliced into the ground. An instant later, the beast was nearly cut in half by Anna's counter-attack. She had dropped the gun and seized the captured weapon, and now wielded it with deadly accuracy.

A few feet away, Chuck was also fending off a close attack, but managed to drop two of the predators, as Ashley fired from his flank. In a moment it was over, the predators beating a quick retreat. The victim of Anna's blow didn't move.

"Mosely!" she screamed, when her thoughts cleared. "Are you ok?"

He was lying on the ground, his revolver emptied at the retreating beasts, and he fumbled for more cartridges as he replied. "It got my leg. I don't know if I can stand."

Anna quickly knelt to examine the wound. "It's pretty deep, Mosely, like a big smile in the back of your calf," she told him, "but it's not bleeding. I think the weapon cauterized it."

"So now I know why it's burning like fire," he told her. "At least it's still attached, right?"

"Yes, but we need to get you to a doctor," she told him. "We don't have any bandages to cover the wound. You need to be stitched up."

Chuck remained standing, watching to be sure that the retreat was genuine. Convinced at last, he quickly pulled out his knife and sliced six inches off the bottom of his long overcoat. "It's not sterile, but maybe you can wrap it in this, and pull the wound closed."

Sarah stood breathlessly watching, unsure what she could do to help, then thought of the twine that had been wound around the rifle before. "Here, use some of this," she said. "You can tie it around the cloth."

As Anna attended to Mosely, he finished reloading, and was scanning the darkness for new attacks.

Chuck stood sentry for the next few minutes, his eyes in constant motion. "Sarah, let me have your light for a moment," he said.

Sarah quickly handed him the floodlight, and he flicked it on and swept it across the landscape. "They're huddled up only a hundred yards away, I think," he told the group. "I can see some faint movement out there, and I doubt it's pronghorns or cattle. They're too smart to hang around these creatures. I can't tell if they're planning to try to rush us again, but we need to be ready." He swept the light one more pass around. "It looks like they abandoned those rocks ahead. Do you think we can move Mose that far?" he asked.

"Just tell me where you want me," Mosely spoke up. "I ain't dead yet. I'll get me there."

"You can't just hop up and walk on that," Anna told him. "Maybe If you lean on me and use me as a crutch you can move."

"Well, it hurts bad enough lying down, I can't imagine it will be much worse moving," he told her. "Let's give it a try."

"Here," said Sarah, bending to pick up the fallen scimitar. "Wish it to turn off, then use it as a crutch."

"Thanks, Sarah," Mosely said as they helped him off the ground. "It's not far, right?"

"A couple of hundred feet," Chuck told him as he continued to search their surroundings. "I'm hoping we can find a bit of defense there among the rocks."

Together the small band began to move through the heavy snow, Chuck breaking a path, Mosely limping badly in the center despite Anna's help, and Sarah bringing up the rear with her reloaded rifle. "Anything you see raise its head, go ahead and shoot it," Chuck told her. "Keep them away until we get settled in, then we can fight 'em up close again if we have to, where the revolvers can do more damage."

Ten minutes later they had Mosely seated, propped against one of three large boulders at the foot of the talus slope. The stones gave them some defense, despite the size of the attackers. "Stay close," Chuck told them, "and try to conserve your heat. It's going to get colder before the sun comes up again."

With a sudden deceleration the car they were riding in slowed to a halt, and the three of them carefully scanned the transportation hub before emerging. It seemed vacant.

"Well, so far, so good," Tom said. "I hope we gave them the shake for a while. They were getting too close for comfort."

"The trick will be to get another machine going before they can catch us," Jason said. "I'm hoping that they will be afraid of it and will leave us alone once it's started."

"If they were afraid of the cleaning machine, which they must see fairly often, there's no telling how they will react to a machine they've never seen before," Ashley said.

"Right, but that's assuming it still works after, what, a thousand years or so?" Tom said. "What if we get down there and there is no machine, or it won't start? We'll be trapped in the basement with no hope of escape, no food, little water, and limited ammunition."

"Yeah, there's that," Jason admitted, "but we've managed to stay ahead of them so far, and this still seems like our best chance to escape. If it doesn't work, we go to plan 'B.'"

"What's plan 'B'?" Ashley asked him as she swiped through the screens again.

"Run," Jason replied seriously.

"I think this is it," Ashley said, pointing at a transportation node. "We need to pass through this place. It's two levels straight down, if I'm reading this correctly."

"Yes, that's exactly right," Jason said. "This board makes a lot more sense to me now. That maze of lines includes ventilation shafts, energy distribution, corridors, ramps, elevators, and horizontal shuttle tunnels. It maps almost everything about this place, but…" he paused. "There's something else in the basement that confuses me. I get a strange feeling about it, like…"

"Like what?" Ashley pressed him. "What's strange about the basement, except that there's no exits, that's where these things hang out, and that's where they parked the heavy machinery?"

"There's something more the AI was trying to me. Something about the future."

"I guess we'll find out when we get there," Tom said. "Let's be moving, I don't like waiting in one place very long, and I think I hear something coming."

As before, Ashley reached with her captured weapon to select a destination, and they boarded the waiting lift. In a few seconds they had descended to the second level, and in moments made the transition to another lateral transport. When they cautiously exited, they found the cavernous space empty.

"OK, now all we have to do is find the ramp that runs down from here," Tom said. "That shouldn't be too hard."

"Not if it's like the place we were in before on this level," Jason replied, already turning toward where he suspected it would be. "I think that's it," he said, pointing.

They made their way toward the dark opening, checking for further possible ambushes, but found nothing out of the ordinary.

"Let's head down," Tom said, "and hope we don't have to fight our way back up."

"You've become a bit of a pessimist, Dad," Jason chided. "Let's just see if that AI was steering me straight. If it was, we're nearly home."

"We still have no idea how fast that thing can cut through this rock, son," Tom said. "If it takes it a week to make a new exit, it won't do us a bit of good."

"Still, we've come this far," Ashley said. "We've got to try."

Together the three of them began the long decent of the curving ramp, Jason taking the lead, and Tom acting as the rearguard. Jason continually peered around the long curve as the tunnel lighted in response to their presence. "The way still looks clear," he told them, "and I think I see the room at the bottom."

At last they exited into another large hall, again featuring the same curved shape. The adjacent shaft was nearby, and Ashley boldly peeked into it. "We're near the bottom," she reported. "It only goes another fifty feet or so lower, but it's a very long way back up. I don't see any light up there, but I hear…something. Maybe a waterfall?"

"That's the predators," Jason said. "Let's get busy and find the machine."

"Hey, there's a doorway over there," Tom said. "Maybe that's the garage they parked this thing in?"

"Let's see," Ashley said, and approached the opening.

"Wait," said Jason. "Let's check this out first." He peered carefully around the corner. "It's a long hall of some sort, with lots of dividers," he said. "I doubt it's where the machine is, but it has some sort of special purpose…I'd like to know…"

Suddenly the air was split by a high-pitched screaming, and they realized it was coming from the room before them. As Jason watched, a half-sized predator ran away from the doorway shrieking, heading deeper into the room. Its cries were immediately answered by a chorus of ear-splitting screeches and screams.

"We've started something not good," Tom said.

Jason stood transfixed as two larger predators, both unarmed, advanced from the interior of the long hall, and stood blocking the central corridor that divided the room. The screaming continued all around them.

"I think we need to leave this area," Jason said. "The pack will be here fast now. And I think I know what we've stumbled upon."

"What?" Ashley demanded, as they began to run away from the doorway and farther through the main hall. "What was that place, and why didn't they attack?"

"They were unarmed. They normally are, because they were nannies. That's the nursery," he said.

"Lord knows we don't need to get these things any more agitated than they already are about us," Tom said. "And I don't know about you, but I didn't come down here with the idea of wiping out baby any-things."

"I'm with you," Jason said. "Let's just get out of here now!"

They dashed along the corridor but saw no sign of machinery. "Where do you suppose they hid this thing we're looking for," Ashley said. "We need to find it quick, because I think I hear something coming up behind us."

"There must be a side compartment, like that cleaning machine was in," Jason said. 'Watch along the walls for any sort of deviation, a door, a panel, anything that might indicate an opening."

"There, up ahead," Tom said. "Is that a door?"

Jason sprinted ahead and arrived at what seemed to be a metallic panel, a slightly different color from the rest of the walls. "I think this could be it, but I don't see any sort of controls," he told them as they caught up.

"Do what you did before," Ashley said. "Touch it. Order it to open."

Jason did as she suggested, and immediately the door began to slide away. Beyond was a massive horizontal tube of metal, devoid of any sort of feature or opening. "It just looks like a piece of pipe," Ashley said. "How can we use that to get out? It doesn't even seem to have a door."

"Wait," said Jason. "Let's try." He walked up to the smooth blue metal object and placed his hand upon it. In a moment it responded by displaying a glowing panel which suddenly appeared on the side.

Ashley reached out and touched the surface of the metal. "It's cold. It feels like steel or something, but it's slick. So how is it that we can see that panel, and a three-dimensional display, in solid metal?"

"How did they make those other displays in solid rock?" Jason replied. "Obviously they have way better technology than we do."

Jason was already manipulating the panel, sweeping his hand and touching each new display that appeared.

"Do you know what you're doing, or just guessing?" Tom asked, his eyes on the door behind, where they could hear the growing sound of commotion.

"I think I know, but it's like an instinct, because I sure can't read all these marks or instructions," he replied. "I just hope this works." As he finished speaking a thin crack appeared, and seemed to grow, splitting the solid metal finish of the tube. Seconds later, a door recessed and swung inward. They peeked cautiously inside, and they could see a spartan interior, and a bank of panels, similar to what they had seen throughout the complex. Just then, a rising tumult and the pattering of dozens of feet announced the arrival of the pack of predators, closing in fast.

"Quick, get in, it's our only option now, anyway," Jason said, and the three of them piled in, tumbling onto a plain metal floor.

"Now how do we close the door?" Ashley asked. "They're almost here!"

Jason was already at the panels before him, and once again they lighted in holographic displays. "Please hurry, Jason!" Ashley said, her voice rising into a panic. "They're here!"

Suddenly the machine beneath them gave a rumble, which rose quickly to a whine. Outside the tumult seemed to halt. Tom risked a peek. "They've stopped, I think. You may be right, they are afraid of this, too, at least for the moment."

"Stand clear of the door," Jason said. "I think we're going for a ride!"

The machine suddenly lurched, and a loud roar drowned out all conversation.

Chapter Thirty-Two

MOSELY GRIMACED AS HE LAY ON THE GROUND, his revolver still gripped in his hand. He peered around the bottom edge of the boulder covering the eastern approaches to their rocky redoubt. Behind him, Chuck faced the broadest opening, the most likely point of attack. Between the two, Sarah had her rifle braced atop a rock, aimed up the ridge toward the invisible enemy.

Anna still held the captured scimitar but had momentarily set it down to fumble with the knotted twine that Sarah had produced from her pocket. As she completed her project she held it aloft and proudly announced "It's not much, but it might buy us some time if it gets hairy. Behold the torch."

Chuck turned long enough to catch a glimpse of the crude affair, nothing more than a few score twists of twine around a bough of 'lighter' pine kindling. "I hope we don't need it, but I'm glad you have it," he said.

"I wish we could build a fire, myself," Anna said, "but if there's any more wood around here, it's under all this snow."

"A fire would be nice," Mosely said, "and a shot of whiskey might help dull this pain. It's starting to hurt pretty bad now," he added.

"Hang in there, partner," Chuck replied. "Dawn will be coming around in less than an hour, and I think the advantage shifts to that rifle as soon as it's light enough to see these critters. We're going to get you home safe and sound."

"Um, Chuck, I think I see something," Sarah said. "There's some shapes on the left, and on the right too."

"Yeah, I see 'em too," Mosely said. "Get ready, they're going to rush us again."

"Take the rifle and go ahead and pop one, Sarah, if you have a clear shot," Chuck said. "Maybe that will make 'em reconsider."

Sarah aimed at one of the distant shapes and let fly a round. "They all ducked," she reported. "At least they've learned to fear the guns."

"I wonder why they're after us, anyway," Anna said. "They've got lots of easier stuff to kill and eat that doesn't shoot back."

"I guess it must be down to a grudge match now," Mosely said. "We got into their place, and shot it up a bit, now they're trying to even the score."

"If they're going to do that, they'll do it soon, 'cause its fixin' to get light soon enough," Chuck said.

"Well, we didn't start this. They got into our place last night, and tried to get to me," Sarah said, "I had to shoot one then."

"They did?" Mosely said. "Where, inside your house?"

"Yeah," Sarah replied. "I didn't know what it was at the time, I thought it was a bear until I saw these things."

"So," Mosely said. "Do you suppose they're after the women? After all, it seems like Tom and Jason may have been trying to get Ashley back when they went down in that tunnel, her being missing from her snowcat and all..."

"Yes, makes sense to me," Chuck said, "but I don't know why they would want them. These ones here are mighty bony and all..."

Sarah and Anna both stifled a grin, surprised that they felt a momentary relief at the comment, which served to break the intense tension they all felt. At any moment, they knew, they might be rushed by an overwhelming number of the beasts.

The eastern sky was just beginning to show a hint of dawn, and the fragile party was hoping that the worst was behind them when their hopes were dashed. "Here they come again," Sarah said. "I can see three or four on each side up the slope."

"I've got at least two coming from down this way," Mosely replied, cocking his revolver to its hair-trigger position.

"Well, this is it, friends. It's do or die," Chuck said. "Aim straight."

"Oh, don't be so damned maudlin, Chuck," Mosely replied. "Just shoot 'em where it hurts, and we'll be alright in the end."

The sudden rush of the beasts drew everyone to lock on a target, and shots began to ring out, but the sheer numbers brought the beasts into their circle. One sprang upon the boulder and crouched insect-like before Mosely put two shots into it from below. Anna blocked another attacker's sweeping swing of a scimitar with her own weapon, and managed to slice a limb from the beast, sending it reeling. Chuck put two slugs in another before it cut him down, and he fell in a heap in the snow. Sarah fired her rifle as fast as she could and dropped another as it leapt over the rocks toward Mosely, who managed to drop a fourth in front of his blazing revolver.

Then, as quickly as it had begun, the beasts fled. Anna shoved eight feet of rubbery arm off herself and rushed to where Chuck lay. "Chuck, are you alright?" she asked. He groaned, and she rolled him over. There was a gash that cut through his coat and shirts, slicing across his chest. He was breathing but seemed to be in shock.

"What made 'em run away?" Mosely asked. "I thought we were all goners."

"I don't know," Sarah said, "but I'm glad they did. Chuck's hurt pretty bad."

"What's that sound?" Anna suddenly said, looking up from tending to Chuck's wound. A sudden rumble seemed to shake the ground around them and grow steadily louder. A few seconds passed before the sound grew to a roar. Moments later, only a few hundred yards away, the ground seemed to burst open and spew out a large metal cylinder.

Chapter Thirty-Three

THE SIGHT OF ASHLEY, JASON, AND TOM emerging from the huge machine brought a cheer from Sarah, and raised the spirits of Mosely and Chuck, both braced against rocks in the early morning light. A wave of relief swept over the whole group as they sensed that the nightmare was ending.

"We've got to get these men to a doctor, right away," Anna told them after a brief round of greetings. "They both have serious wounds that need to be stitched up."

"Jason, do you think you can make it to the house, get some fuel, and get Ashley's snowcat going again?" Tom asked. "There's no other way we'll be able to get these men back there in less than a few hours."

"Sure, Dad. I've got enough ammo to defend myself, and I doubt those things will come back in broad daylight. They never have before."

"Oh!" Ashley said, reaching into the pocket of her coat. "Here's the key! I've had it along all this time!"

Jason took the key and started off toward the house, plowing through the foot of snow that blocked his path. "That will take him an hour, anyway," Anna said. "Isn't there something we can do for these men?"

"I'll be fine, take care of Chuck there," Mosely said.

"I'm hurting plenty, but I'll live," Chuck answered.

"The wound goes to the bone, but no farther," Anna told Tom. "They were both very lucky."

Tom nodded back at the remains of the monstrous attacker that they had passed walking from the machine. "If that's any indication of what those weapons do, they should thank their lucky stars. Who did that?"

"I did," Anna said. "It was trying to kill Mosely, so I really had no choice."

Tom looked admiringly at Anna. "Don't feel bad, it had it coming. You know, for a school teacher, you can sure surprise."

Anna smiled at Tom, and despite her fatigue, her face was aglow in the morning light. "I've still got a few more up my sleeve, if you care to stick around," she told him.

Tom was smiling back, a mischievous gleam in his eye. "I think it's you that should consider sticking around. Do you think you could ever consider a change of lifestyle?"

Anna paused only a moment. "I've been thinking about that question for a few months now, actually," she said. "But give me a few more days, and we can discuss it again. Let's get ourselves to safety, first."

"Dad!" came a shout from Jason, already a hundred yards away. "There's something happening up there!"

Turning toward the cliffs, Tom was stunned to see a moving mass partway up the face of the mountain. It seemed to be slowly descending. Toward them.

"What do you make of that?" Mosely said, trying to shift himself to get a better view.

"I hate to tell you, but it looks like they're coming back," Tom said. "Unless my eyes are playing tricks on me, it looks like a hundred or so predators." He turned and shouted to Jason. "Come back here! You can't face them alone!"

Jason turned and hurried back toward the others.

"Everyone be sure you've got guns loaded, and spare ammunition at hand," Tom told them. "This will be the fight of our lives."

"I wish't I had my field glasses," Mosely said. "I can see 'em, just not clear enough. What do you suppose made 'em come out in the open, in daylight like this? Just to get us?"

"That does seem strange," Tom said.

Jason came huffing up and paused only a moment before he panted, "I don't think they're coming to attack us."

"Why?" Anna asked. "What makes you think otherwise?"

"I think I can see little ones," Jason said. "They have the babies along with them."

Tom turned his attention back to the greenish cluster, which had gathered at the top of the talus slope. "I can't see that much detail, but you've got better eyes. It does look like they stopped moving, though. That still doesn't explain what they're doing out."

"Dad, I think I might know. Remember how they ran from the cleaning machine? Maybe this was just their reaction to the noise of our digger."

"There's something else going on, too," Ashley said, pointing. "What's that?"

All heads turned as she pointed skyward. Above the cliffs, a ripple seemed to move through the sky. It steadily approached the top of the plateau. "That looks almost like a tornado!" Sarah said, pointing to a spot below it. A sudden swirl of objects was flying into the air.

Above, the ripple began to assume a more defined shape. "It's masked, like the sphere was," Jason said. "I think it's a ship!"

"It's huge," Anna said. "I think it's going to land on the plateau."

"Even better," Jason replied. "It's going to land *in* the plateau. I finally understand what those huge shafts were for."

As they watched a tall spindle shape emerged, visible only because of the faint distortion that rippled along its edges. Otherwise it perfectly matched the sky behind it. It steadily descended and seemed to pass directly into the mountain.

"Well, I'll be danged," Chuck said. "Do you think it's an invasion?"

"I don't think so," Jason replied. "It's more like a rescue party."

The group remained on silent guard another few minutes, watching the clustered predators on the slope above them. Nothing seemed to move as the warming sun slowly broke higher into the sky.

"Jason, I think there's someone here that wants to speak to you," Ashley said softly. He turned to see a large sphere hovering only a few feet away. He turned to face it, and again a light seemed to sparkle from its surface and focus on Jason. He stood still for a long moment, and the light faded.

"They are here to assist," Jason said. "They are offering to transport Mosely and Chuck to safety for us. They want me to follow them." As he spoke, the large sphere seemed to divide, and a smaller faint sphere appeared beside it.

"Get ready, men, you are going to be levitated," Jason said. Moments later, the two men seemed to slowly and gently rise, hovering three feet from the ground.

"Well, I can't believe my eyes," Tom said.

"It doesn't hurt," Mosely said. "I feel like I'm lying on a pillow."

The two men began to move slowly in the direction of the house. Anna and Sarah quickly fell in behind. "You'd better go, too, Dad," Jason said. "I've got a bit of business still to attend to."

"Where are you going, Jason?" Ashley asked. "Will you be safe?"

"I don't know if this is what you would choose, Ashley, but they want you to come along with me."

She paused only a moment. "Where are we going?" she asked.

"Back into the maze," he replied.

Chapter Thirty-Four

"**I** FINALLY GOT THROUGH to the sheriff's office," Tom told the group gathered in the living room of the C9 ranch house. "They're sending an air ambulance. You guys are going to get a helicopter ride."

Anna and Sarah were applying bandages to the two wounded cowboys, who seemed to be in good spirits despite their injuries. "Another first for me," Mosley said from his place on a sofa. "First, I get to fight aliens, and now I get to fly. I still think I got the better of 'em."

"That you did, Mose," Chuck chimed in from the facing sofa. "You showed 'em what you were made of."

"Yeah, they got a closer look at that than I intended, though," he said, and got chuckles from the group.

"It's such a relief to be back in this house, and to have that sphere standing guard," Sarah said, nodding toward the window, where the faintly-visible shape still hovered.

"Yeah, what a strange way to get home," Tom said. "But I'm still worried about Jason and Ashley. I wonder why they were called back?"

"I can't believe she agreed to go back down in that hole!" Sarah said. "That's more than a little bit brave, don't you think?"

"She's a special woman," Tom said, and Mosely and Chuck both added their agreement.

"Hopefully we'll be back working for her in a couple of weeks," Chuck said.

"Let's just hope that's the case, Chuck," Tom said, staring out the window toward the edge of the cliffs. "Hey, the pack of predators on the mountain is gone!" he suddenly exclaimed.

•

Ashley and Jason turned back to the west, retracing their own footprints in the snow. "Hey!" Ashley exclaimed, "the machine's gone!"

Jason looked to see the hole they had created, and nothing more than the imprint of the heavy machine amid the rock and debris they had cast aside. "They took it back already," Jason said. "I think they are going to be putting other things to right, too," he added.

Together they walked down the gently-sloping tunnel they had created only an hour earlier, led by a faintly-glowing sphere. "I'm scared, Jason," Ashley said, and slipped her hand into his.

"Don't worry, I'm going to make sure you're safe. I don't think the sphere would lead us back down here if there were any danger." He gave her hand a squeeze and refused to let go.

Twenty minutes later they passed though the garage they had burrowed through on their way out and turned into the main hall. They passed the nursery, now silent and empty. A short walk beyond they found themselves back in the curved transportation hub. "Look, the shaft is gone!" Ashley whispered to Jason.

"It's occupied," he said, looking at the metallic skin of the craft that stood in the former opening. "It was the docking port. All those levels correspond to the compartments of the ship."

"That's pretty brilliant," Ashley said, but clung tight to Jason's arm. "But if it's a ship, who's ship is it, and are they dangerous?"

"If I thought for a minute that it was, we wouldn't be standing here," Jason replied. "Let's just see what they want."

A moment later a large panel slid away, revealing a tall port in the vessel. Then a short ramp extended to span the slender gap between the ship and the platform. Ashley drew a gasp when a human stepped through the portal and turned to face them, smiling. He walked two steps toward them and stopped at a respectful distance.

"I am Hologato," he said. "I am here to apologize to you and your people, on behalf of the Sormalian race, my own people, and the Gorneans, as well."

"You speak English?" Jason asked, surprised.

"It is not my first language," the man replied. "I am a linguist and translator and have studied it for many years. We can monitor this world from our own."

"Who are these people you speak of?" Jason asked him.

"Do not be afraid, I will introduce you," he said.

He turned toward the door and gestured. Through the opening came a slender, apparently armless figure more than fifteen feet tall. It seemed not to walk at all, but merely floated toward them, and halted beside Hologato. "This is my friend, Sorshunamabar," he said.

"I am Jason, and this is my friend, Ashley," Jason replied uncertainly.

"It is a pleasure to meet you," Ashley said boldly. The tall figure made a sort of bow, and then a strange sound seemed to emanate from it..

"Sorshunamabar is a representative of the Sormalians," Hologato explained, "and the commander of this vessel. He apologizes, both for the injury done by the Gorneans, and for his lack of knowledge of English. They have always communicated with my people through spirit, what you might call telepathy. We have no need for words."

"Who are they Gorneans?" Jason asked, a bit overwhelmed.

"They are the race of people who have caused you injury. Their leader also wishes to apologize for the actions of their kin," Hologato said. He beckoned once more, and through the door stepped a massive predator, very much like those they had been locked in combat with only hours earlier. Four tree-like legs carried the creature, and four thick arms were folded across its crown. The strange jaws that topped the creature were somehow retracted into its body. It made a strange barking sound, and Ashley's grip on Jason's arm grew vise-like, but she stood her ground.

"This is my friend, Gorgatho. He is a leader among his race. He also offers his apologies."

Jason stared at the creature, looking up at the double row of eyes that encircled its trunk and seemed to be regarding him in return. "Um…" he stammered. "I am sorry that our people were in conflict," he said diplomatically.

Hologato quickly translated and turned back to Jason and Ashley. "You are not to be blamed. He will deal with the transgressors. His people are already boarding this ship and will be removed from this world."

"But, you, Hologato. How did you come to be on this ship?" Ashley asked.

"I was born on a distant world," he answered. "My people and theirs have been friends for many lifetimes. My people came from this place. They once lived in these cliffs and mesas and learned the spirit language of our friends the Sormalians. We traveled with them and now we belong to other, scattered worlds. In time, your people may come to understand, and assume your own place. Until then, may you live in peace," he said, and turned to go.

"But, wait," Ashley started. "You can't just leave without explaining all of this to us. We deserve to understand…"

"It is not time that you should know more," Hologato said to her "Perhaps the time will come soon, but that day is not today."

Jason and Ashley stood in silence as the trio re-boarded their ship, and the ramp was retracted. The portal closed silently, and the ship seemed to simply fade from view. Jason stepped forward and reached out his hand, and felt the smooth, cool surface of the ship, even though it looked as though he was reaching toward vacant space.

"It's masked," he said to Ashley. "We can't really see it, but it's still right here."

The two turned to go, still in awe of what they had witnessed. Then there was a sudden breath of wind from behind them, and they realized that the shaft was truly empty. They looked up the shaft and saw daylight as the vessel departed, then the top of the shaft was suddenly covered.

"It looks like they put the stone back on top!" Jason said. "I hope they got all their friends this time!"

"Let's get out of here," Ashley said. "Just in case."

The two left the maze and the incredible scene they had witnessed, walking in silence back toward the ranch house. As they walked, they heard a sudden rumble and felt a tremor. Jason pointed toward the cliff where he had found the tunnel. "Look, there's some dust drifting down there," he said.

"I think I know what just happened," Ashley told him. "They closed the book on this place, by destroying what they had built inside the mountain. They've probably collapsed all the tunnels."

Jason stood staring at the mountain for a long moment. "I think you're right," he said at last. "It makes sense. They didn't really expect them to be found, and honestly, if those 'Gornean' creatures hadn't gotten hungry enough to rustle our cattle, we probably would never have had a clue that the mountain was hollow."

"You realize that it will never be the same around here again," Ashley said as they resumed their walk. "We can't un-see any of this, you and I, and that goes for Tom and Anna, and Mosely and Chuck, too. Our lives have been changed forever."

"You're right, but you and I are privileged with information that no one else on this planet is apt to know," Jason replied. "I don't think those beings would have come back but for our contact with the sphere. I think that it was only trying to cover tracks when it stole the skull I found."

"I guess it wasn't really your skull to keep," Ashley said. "Look, there's a helicopter at the house!"

"That must be a medivac chopper for Mosely and Chuck. I hope they're going to be OK," Jason said.

"I'm worried about you, too," Ashley told him, still clinging to his hand. "How are you doing after all you've been through?"

"Ashley, if all I ever have for the rest of my life is this moment, then I can say yes, I'm going to be just fine." He pulled her close and kissed her, and she wrapped her arms around his neck.

"Babe, if you can kiss like that," she whispered, "we're set for life."

Acknowledgments

I gratefully dedicate this tale to my patient wife, Susan, who has not only tolerated my many hours spent creating stories but also serves as a very-talented Chief Editor and has been by my side each step of the way.

Special thanks go also to Paul Comkowycz and Grace Engholm, my faithful critics and beta readers.

Thanks also to Plumeria Publishing for taking the stress out of the process of bringing a book to print.

I'd also like to especially thank the many readers who encourage me by buying my books, and those who inspire me, especially my childhood heroes, the writers who wove their eye-opening stories of theoretical distant worlds and the only reliable one, lying just beneath our feet.

Other titles by Robert James Connors:

Non-fiction:

<u>Romancing Through Italy</u>

Compiling the true stories of twenty years spent exploring the cradle of modern civilization, <u>Romancing Through Italy</u> is an intensely-personal love affair with an entire country. From the canals of Venice to the isolated hilltop villages of Abruzzo, stories of Italy's many charms and wonders will leave you wanting to see them all. The wonders of ancient Rome, the Renaissance, modern Italy, and the heroics of Allied soldiers in WWII come to life on the pages.

Coming Soon:

Fiction:

<u>Legend of the Clouds:</u>

      <u>Enigma at Sheltey Island</u>

Historical Fiction:

<u>Booker's Box (the Stories of Florida)</u>

© 2018 Robert James Connors

About the Author

Robert James Connors was born in Chicago, Illinois, the eldest son of a CTA train motorman. He was raised in Florida and began work as a newspaper carrier at age eleven and joined his school newspaper in high school, where he displayed his passion for the written word. He was hired as a full-time news reporter before his graduation, only later enrolling in Barry University to study English.

A former magazine managing editor, journalist, newspaper editorial writer, and author, he has more than 1,000 published human-interest stories, features, and commentaries. He is a contributor to publications covering topics ranging from environment to politics, classical music to history.

Connors is an experienced public speaker, a former Florida county commissioner, and self-taught speaker of Italian. He has served as an invited guest speaker (in both English and Italian) at military commemorative events in Italy, recognizing the service of American and Allied veterans of World War Two in the Liberation of Italy from the Nazi/Fascists. When not traveling, he resides with his wife, Susan, in Lake Wales, Florida.

Follow Robert on Twitter: @R_James_Connors

Robert James Connors

Encounter at Cloud Ranch

Robert James Connors

www.ingramcontent.com/pod-product-compliance
Lightning Source LLC
Chambersburg PA
CBHW050935120626
46552CB00001B/217